Pumpkins and Hearts

By

Mary L. Ball

"For nothing is secret, that shall not be made manifest; neither [any thing] hid, that shall not be known and come abroad"
Luke 8:17

. . ❧ . .

Scriptures from the King James Bible

'PUMPKINS AND HEARTS' is dedicated to my grandson, Blake. He has a wonderful imagination and is always sharing story ideas. Blake's encouragement to write a book that included some aspect of Thanksgiving inspired me to create this story.

I hope you enjoy this fictional tale about Matt's past mistakes, his present anxiety, and the liberation he receives from opening his heart to believe.

. . ❧ . .

CHAPTER ONE

Matt approached the thirty-five-mile speed zone, slowed his luxury car and glanced toward Mason Street. His foot automatically hit the brake, less than a second later he pressed the gas pedal and sped past the intersection, a swash of melancholy sounded. *Sonya's gone, like so many other things.* He looked across the street. Orange and yellow hues cloaked the Sourwood trees. Autumn ascended on North Carolina, and the countryside was ripe with a patchwork of colors.

A vacant building caught his eye. *Burger Bucket.* A vision of the once thriving teen hangout emerged. Matt continued toward the outskirts of town. A mile passed while he considered the path his life had taken. What would be different if he'd stayed in Black Mountain? He should have, after all he could write from anywhere.

His GPS announced a right-turn onto Harper Avenue. According to the directions the rental unit was just ahead. He never considered leasing a tiny house, but the online pictures suited him. The place had several big windows and overlooked a large pumpkin patch. Certainly a different setting from the Washington penthouse he'd called home for a little over five years.

It had been months since he'd written a constructive paragraph. *Find a change of scenery.* The side of his lips turned down as he recalled his agent's words. "Rejuvenate your imagination. Finish the final book of your murder mystery series by Thanksgiving or future contracts might be in danger." *Yeah, I'd fix my writer's block, if I had a magic wand.*

He pulled into the driveway and stopped. White siding gleamed in the sunlight with shutters decorating the windows that matched the green metal roof. He turned off his engine as a little girl ran inside.

Matt stepped out and stretched. After the six hour drive with only a half dozen stops, he could guess what a pretzel felt like.

The sun blocked his view. Matt pulled his sunglasses from his pocket and adjusted them as he watched a woman approach. He sized her up, noting she was a few inches shorter than him. He rubbed his chin. Five foot nine, if his guess was right. She greeted him with a smile.

"You must be Matt Blake." She put her hand out. "I'm Lucinda Wise."

"Pleased." He eyed her black shiny hair that made him think of a Raven.

"Here's the key to your tiny house. It's stocked with dishes and has all the normal amenities of a big home, even has a small flat screen."

"Thanks." He took the key. The essence of her eyes hypnotized him. He'd seen blue waters. The Mediterranean Sea paled in comparison. He briefly looked away, determined not to be swayed by a pretty face. "I don't plan on watching much TV. I'm seeking solitude to jump start my creativity. If everything is ready I'll get settled."

"Sure." Lucinda turned then paused and looked back. "The fridge is located under the sink. The only thing I stocked was bottled water, not knowing what you preferred. If you need anything let me know. We aren't formal around here."

"I'll go into town in a while and get a few items." He mumbled.

Matt got back in his car and steered past the house toward the quarters that he planned to call home for the next two months.

He grabbed his suitcase and entered. He came face to face with a sink, and a minuet counter. He gaped at the micro size quarters. Seeing it online romanticized the shelter. *What was I thinking?* The end of the three hundred square feet, fashioned a door, which led into the bath and a narrow flight of stairs that made the loft accessible. To his left, a chair joined a fold-down table. Three wide long windows offered a view over the field. He leaned back on his heels and looked beyond to the gold and red countryside. The scenery was what he'd paid for.

Matt unpacked and found a space big enough to accommodate four clothes hangers. He took the stairs to his sleeping quarters. At least, the lady made the room cozy. He lay on the mattress to test its softness.

A broken melody of "Ring around the Roses" woke him. He listened to the singing, peered out of the long peep hole in the loft and saw a little girl. Matt took the stairs with caution. The sun was going down and a child was outside skipping around in the dusk of the day. He squeezed his eyes shut and opened them again. "Isn't it too dark for the child to play?" He stepped on the door stoop. "Hey, why aren't you inside? It's getting late."

"Sorry Mister. I forgot." The little girl swung back and forth. Brown eyes, huge with surprise, focused on him.

"Come on." Matt huffed and lightly touched the child's back. "Let's take you back home, where you belong."

. . ❧ . .

"FAITH." LUCINDA'S VOICE rose as she searched the room. "Honey, where are you?"

"If this is Faith, I found her." Matt's voice echoed from the patio through the back door which connected with the kitchen.

Lucinda hurried. "There you are!" She took Faith's hand. "Thank you. I told her to wash up for dinner."

"It's getting dark." Matt tilted his head toward the sky. "I'm not a parent. Still, I don't think a little girl needs to be out at this time of the evening."

"Mister Blake." She narrowed her eyes. "I can assure you that I don't let her roam in the dark."

"Mommy, I was looking for the pumpkins." Lucinda's shirt tail pulled from Faith's nudge.

"I'm sorry she bothered you." She glanced at Matt, then back to her daughter. "Honey, remember, I told you earlier, the crop is still small."

"Mister, you can stay and eat with us. Mommy always fixes a lot of food."

"I doubt that's a good idea." As he tried to ignore the aroma of baked chicken he watched the child put her finger in her mouth, and then removed it.

"Mister Blake, I don't mean to be nosy. I didn't see you go anywhere. Do you have groceries?" She pushed up her shirtsleeve.

"Not yet. I fell off to sleep." The corners of his eyes crinkled. "Thank you, for the comfortable sleeping area."

"I see." Lucinda nodded. "Faith is right. We have plenty. Perhaps, you'll join us. Tomorrow you can go to the store."

Matt turned his attention from Lucinda to the child as the smell of home cooking enticed his taste buds. "I don't suppose it would hurt anything. You both should call me Matt."

"Very well, Matt... I'm Lucinda. And you've met Faith." She touched the child's hair. "Make yourself at home. I'll get the table ready."

He stepped inside and Faith grasped his hand. "Come on, I'll show you my gerbil. His name is Mickey."

The rodent spun its wheel around. After a few seconds, Matt moved away from the hold the child had on him and eyed her. Children were something that intrigued him from a distance and for research purposes. His notions about the little girl halted when Lucinda's voice beckoned. "Dinner is ready you guys."

Matt frowned, *you guys. What a way to announce a meal.*

He took the seat that Lucinda indicated. "Everything looks good." Matt placed a paper napkin on his lap.

"Thank you. It's rotisserie chicken."

Matt expected Lucinda to offer him a serving dish with the main course, or the bread basket. Instead, she smiled and bowed her head.

"Heavenly Father, we thank you for this meal and ask you to watch over us. Amen."

Before he opened his eyes he heard Faith's small voice repeat the affirmation.

"This is a nice house." He scanned the kitchen that was adjacent to the dining area. He figured small talk was needed, even if it wasn't his strongest talent.

"I like it. The yard is just the right size for me to maintain. At times, the grounds can get a bit out of hand. I hire someone with a tractor for that." Her eyes twinkled with response before she handed Faith a roll.

"Why do you call this place The Pumpkin Farm?" He scooped a helping of potatoes.

"It's what I do." Lucinda offered Matt the dish of green beans, "When I'm not doing the books for several companies around town."

"You work for an accountant?" Matt savored the sauce. His taste buds appreciated the sweet brown sugar and onion mixture.

"No, I work from home. I'm blessed to have my own clients." She picked up her glass. "It makes it easy to be with Faith. At least, until she starts kindergarten next year."

"I'm five." The child chimed in.

"Really." Matt glanced Faith's way and saw her push a strip of chicken in her mouth. "I would have thought you'd be in school already."

"I go next year." The little girl swallowed her food and shook her head. "Mom says my birthday didn't come at the right time." She twisted her face unsure.

"I see." Matt opened his roll and added butter.

"Mister, I mean Matt." Faith pushed her plate back. "Whatcha do for money?"

He heard Lucinda gasp and held up his hand. "It's fine. It's good to be inquisitive. I'm a writer." He shook his head and smiled at the child.

"Whatcha write?" She placed her small hands on the side of her face.

"I write stories." He sipped the last of his beverage.

"Why did you come here?" She put her chin in her hand. "Can't you write at your house?"

"Faith!" Lucinda pressed her lips together, and then sighed. She turned to the child. "Honey, Matt is on vacation. Go feed your gerbil." She pushed her hair back as faith jogged out of the room. "Would you like a slice of apple pie? They're fresh from my tree." Lucinda added.

"I can't turn it down."

"I'm sorry about Faith's questions. Sometimes she's too nosy."

"A young person's curiosity can make a person uncomfortable. I suppose it shows the child is thirsty for knowledge." He paused and ran his hand through his hair. "I'm hoping to rejuvenate my thought process. My agent advised me to take some R&R." He shot Lucinda a half grin and wondered why he admitted his problem.

"What was your last book titled?"

"Washington Maze."

"You're Matt Hew, the author! I've read the Washington Chronicle series." Lucinda put her finger up. "I'll be right back."

She returned with two books and a pen. "I hope you don't mind autographing these."

"Not at all. I'm glad you're a fan." He signed the novels. "What did you think?"

"Well..." Lucinda stacked the paperbacks on top of each other. "Honestly, I read the first book, Washington Stairs, years ago and got hooked on the series because of the setting." She shook her head. Washington Maze, I have to admit that I skipped to the last chapter to see who the killer was." She frowned. "You'll get back on the right track."

"Please." Matt laid his hand over hers. Then, as if the touch shocked him, he pulled away. "I want your opinion about the last one."

"The story wasn't insightful or suspenseful like the others. I don't read your books for the crime. I enjoy plots based around the Capitol." She leaned her chin on her hand. "The first novels lets the reader get a sense of the inside workings of Washington politics, and the pencil pushers. "This one." She pushed the book close. "Didn't appeal to me that much." She paused a second. "I'm sorry."

Matt's eyes widened. "It's fine. I asked. I hate to admit I lacked a little enthusiasm. That's why I'm here." He rubbed his neck. "For some reason, I've lost the pleasure of creating a story."

"So you thought coming to small town America would help. Why Black Mountain, North Carolina? It's a far cry from Washington DC."

"I grew up here. I wanted to get back to my roots and rekindle the ambition I used to have. I went to Black Mountain High. I don't recall seeing you there."

"I moved here from Albany, New York. Faith was only a few months old."

"Okay, now it's my turn. Why here?"

"I'd heard a lot of good things about the town and the people. I figured it would be a safe place to raise a child."

"You do a lot of farming on your property?"

"Just my pumpkin patch and a very small apple orchard." She motioned for him to have another piece of pie. "We're busy come harvest time. I've always enjoyed the Thanksgiving holiday. I guess that's why I like growing pumpkins and apples."

"This is delicious. From the website it looks like more than a garden." Matt cut into his second piece of pie.

"I usually plant a couple acres to serve the grocery store in Black Mountain and other customers."

"Wow. You do have a busy life with a child, a career and farming." He moved his empty dish to the side. "I don't mean to pry. Where is your husband?"

. . ❦ . .

LUCINDA PUT THE LID on the pie plate and studied his brown eyes, circles as dark as the fertile ground rested under perfectly arched brows. Her focus fell on his dimpled chin. His handsome face was certainly a distraction for any woman. She nibbled the inside of her jaw. Matt posed the same question that she'd faced when she moved to North Carolina. *People think what they want.* She frowned. A Bible verse from 2 Corinthians 5, played through her mind like background music. "*Therefore if any man be in Christ, he is a new creature: old things are passed away; behold, all things are become new.*"

"I've never been married. It's just me and Faith. Since coming here I've became a Christian. I enjoy a simpler life now." She eyed him and waited for a show of disapproval.

• • ❧ • •

MATT SLID HIS TEETH over his bottom lip. Lucinda's admission of being a single mother from a big city surprised him. She seemed like the average small town, church going lady. He'd even assumed her husband was dead. His writer instincts perked up, sure that there was more to Lucinda Wise, than the people of this mountain town would ever know.

CHAPTER TWO

Matt pushed his chair away from the table. "It looks like you're doing a good job with Faith. This was a wonderful meal, but I should go."

"Wait." Lucinda retrieved a plastic dish from her cupboard. "You might want a snack later." She cut another slice of pie, and then handed it to Matt.

"Thank you." Matt took the dish. His grin grew bigger. "I appreciate the hospitality."

"I'm glad you enjoyed. It's nice to have someone to talk with over dinner. Have a good night, Matt."

He left Lucinda's and continued toward his quarters.

. . ⸎ . .

LUCINDA WATCHED MATT amble across the yard, down the long drive toward the tiny house. She reached for the novels Matt had autographed and carried them back to the shelf.

After getting Faith down for the night, she picked up her phone and tapped the screen.

"Hello." Her friend's greeting, perky as usual.

"Cynthia, if I tell you something will you promise to keep it a secret?"

"Of course I will." A musical giggle sounded. "I'm your daughter's Sunday school teacher."

"I know you're a good person and wouldn't mean to divulge anything." Lucinda flopped down on the ottoman. "This needs to stay between us. Don't even tell James."

"Okay. I won't tell hubby." A sigh flowed through the airwaves. "I promise."

"Remember, when I mentioned that I rented the tiny house to a man from Washington?"

"The man's name is Blake, right?"

"Yes, Matt Blake. Did you know he's from around here?" Lucinda stretched her legs out.

"I didn't grow up in North Carolina." Cynthia's friendly reminder aired.

"Me either, but I found out that not only is he from here. He's the famous author, Matt Hew."

Lucinda waited for a comment and added. "Cynthia, did you hear me?"

"Yes, I've read his books. Why would a big time author like him come back to this little town?"

"To write." Lucinda lowered her voice. "Don't say anything. Folks might pester him."

"I promised. You have to tell me, is he as good-looking as the cover picture on his second book shows?"

"Oh man!" Lucinda moved from the ottoman to her recliner. "Let's see, he's about six foot three, has thick eye-lashes. He must work out. He looks muscular." She continued to describe Matt, painting a picture of his physique for her friend.

• • ❧ • •

THE SUN'S RAYS STEEPED into the windows of the tiny house spilling onto Matt's shoulders and computer. Even though he was relaxed by the warmth of the bright day he still massaged his neck. Stress from his half-finished novel hovered. He clicked on the last manuscript from his series based in the city he lived and pondered over vague notions for his next writing adventure.

Matt surveyed the scenery from his window. His writing reminded him of a lost friendship. If he couldn't get his groove back what then? Writing stories was all he knew. He sipped on his bottle of water. Being in his home town had stirred up his imagination, but so far, it wasn't the creative kind. Scenes of different possibilities that could have happened made him take an uneasy breath. In the distance, he eyed a tall pine. The last day he talked to his old girlfriend, he was submerged in his new career. He took a fast glance toward the blue sky. Sonya was too young to leave this world. He turned away from the view of the countryside, maneuvered the mouse, and clicked on his work-in-progress.

An hour later, he crossed his arms and gave his half empty page a vacant look. A concept struck him, and he started typing, working his character toward the wounded lobbyist. For the next few minutes, the words flowed from his fingers. He typed chapter nineteen and deliberated on the direction he wanted the plot to go. He could wrap it up, if it wasn't for his contracted word count. Briefly, he glanced at the bottom of his document and mentally counted the additional chapters needed.

A progression of loud squeaks blared from out of nowhere. He jumped. More popping and shrill pitches invaded his solitude. He went to the door and looked out. Faith was close by. Her hands squeezed the neck on a balloon. A squelch escaped the rubbery circle, followed by a little girl giggles.

"Hey!" He yelled. "What are you doing playing out here?"

"See my balloon." Faith held up her toy. "I like to make noises with it."

"Well. You need to go home now. I'm trying to work." Matt narrowed his eyes at the child and pointed toward the road where her house stood, three hundred feet away.

"I'm sorry." Faith looked down at her sneakers, turned and ran.

He watched her leave and went back inside to grab his keys. He needed to get groceries. The last thing he had time for was an invitation to dinner, even if Faith's mother was pretty to look at.

• • ❧ • •

LUCINDA LOOKED UP FROM her paperwork. Faith came in rubbing her eyes. "Honey, what's wrong? She motioned for the child to come closer.

"Matt hollered at me."

"Really?" She went to the sink and handed her daughter a glass of water. "Why?"

"I don't know." Faith shrugged. "I was playing beside the tiny house. He yelled and told me to go away."

"I see." Lucinda kneeled and wiped a tear from Faith's cheek. "I'm sure he didn't mean to yell. You should stay in your yard and play. Leave Matt to his peace."

"He can't write books if I make a noise?" Faith's brown eyes widened.

"He's not used to a little girl being around."

"I'll be quieter." Faith looked at the floor.

"Good. Let's forgive Matt for raising his voice." Lucinda hugged her daughter.

• • ❧ • •

MATT FINISHED HIS SANDWICH and cleaned the food preparation area. He spotted the plastic container that held the pie Lucinda had given him. He grabbed it and headed out. If he hurried, he would have time to walk in the field before the sun closed on the day.

He gazed ahead and noticed her on the back deck. Once again the beauty of her hair struck him. The black sheen glistened under the light. The tresses swayed sideways as she gathered a stuffed bear from its resting place on a chair.

"Lucinda, I brought your container back." He handed her the bowl. As she took it their hands touched. Matt ignored the urge to let his fingers linger on her soft skin.

"Thank you." She glanced at the horizon and stepped aside. "It's going to be a beautiful night."

"Yes, it's nice out, even if it is a bit chilly."

"Living in Washington, I'd think you would be comfortable with cold weather."

"Guess I am." Matt grinned and followed Lucinda to a glider. He took a seat beside her. "I was able to get some writing done today."

"That's good." She looked his way sporting a grin.

A bright smile met Matt. For the first time in a while, happiness made him return the grin. She seemed more genuine than most women he had a chance to know, since living in D.C.

"I'm sorry Faith interrupted you today. I told her to play closer to home."

"I may have overreacted. My story was flowing."

"She was crying when she came home."

"Now, it's my turn to apologize." Matt gave the swing a slow push.

"I understand." Lucinda picked at the fur on the teddy. "I'm glad you made progress on your book."

"When I finish this series I believe I'll do some stand-alone stories."

"Will your agent approve?" She stared at him and grinned.

"She should. I did a few before the Washington sequence. I want to back away from run on books for a while."

"I can't imagine the commitment it takes to do those." Lucinda propped her elbow on the top of the lounger arm.

"It's good for readers. They look forward to the next following novel." Matt wiggled his foot as he talked. "I think I'm going through a change. The series seemed to have become mundane for me."

"In Ecclesiastes 3, the first eight stanzas speak of the times we go through." Lucinda pulled her jacket closer. "Verse six says, 'A time to get, and a time to lose; a time to keep, and a time to cast away.' Perhaps, it's your occasion for something different. We all have seasons in our lives."

"That's in the Bible, right?" Matt leaned back.

"Yeah. I quoted the King James Version, the one our church uses. Are you familiar with God's word?"

"Some. I backed away from church when I was in college. When my parents retired to Colorado I stopped going to worship services."

"Matt." She turned sideways. "Why not come with Faith and I to church Sunday?"

"I don't know. I need to spend my time writing."

"It's an open invitation." She stood. "You can think of it as research."

"I'll remember that." Matt got to his feet. "It was nice talking to you." Without thinking about his actions, he reached out and touched her hand.

"Yes, I enjoyed our conversation too. Good night." Lucinda grinned and slid away from his touch.

Matt watched her go inside and then hurried down the path toward his tiny house.

. . ⚜ . .

THE NEXT MORNING MATT'S hair blew astray while he walked around the area. He glanced at the leaves falling. Earlier he'd noticed Lucinda's car back away from the driveway. *Church,* something he'd forgotten. Their conversation the night before made him recall his parents' advice. *Keep the Lord in your life.* It was a saying Mom still quoted from time to time. That, plus she prayed for a change to come in his life. He chuckled. Was prayer as valuable as his mother believed it was? What had Lucinda said, Ecclesiastes? He went inside to his laptop, to search out the verses.

He read the first eight stanzas from the Bible site he'd discovered and opened his writing program. He pasted verse three into the page, along with a few ideas, and reread the scripture. "A time to kill, and a time to heal; a time to break down, and a time to build up."

Matt wiped his mouth and mused over The Holy Word, amazed that something from the Bible could spark a notion for a book. He bookmarked the site and figured he could use it for research, just as Lucinda had suggested.

. . ❧ . .

MATT BREWED HIS MORNING coffee and carried his cup to the table. He booted up his laptop, sipped the hot liquid and savored the rich, roasted flavor. He pointed the curser to his email folder and bypassed messages he planned to read later. The one from his agent got first priority. He glanced at the message. "How's the book?" He typed a quick response and outlined plans for a productive day.

Lunchtime came too fast. He glanced at his watch. Four hours passed, he'd written two chapters, not his usual pace. A year ago, he could have lost himself in the plot and scribe half a novel in such time. Matt's cheeks expanded and deflated with frustration while he searched the field outside.

He'd hoped this would be the answer to his writer's block. *Who am I kidding?* He opened the outline of his story and began to reread a paragraph. In the last week, his summary was the fuel that kept him plowing. He had to get this book finished, no matter how it happened. He began to direct his main character into a trap that he hoped was a believable scheme for a kidnapping.

Matt finished three paragraphs and leaned back in the chair. Mentally drained, he pushed some lose strands of hair from his classic taper cut.

A child's high-pitched voice echoed inside his quarters, followed by a thud. *Faith.* He jumped from his chair and hurried outside. Matt frowned at the little girl squatted on his step. She banged on a plastic car, slamming a rock on the wheel in an attempt to secure it to the frame.

"What are you doing?" He shook his head.

"Stop!" Matt eyed the child and bent down to gather her toy.

"You need to go home. I'm busy."

"Can you?" Faith's request was broken by a labored breath. "Fix my doll's car?" Her small hand pointed to the pink Corvette.

He ran his teeth over his bottom lip prepared to give her the play car and send her away. A tear flowed. Her lips trembled.

Matt looked intently at Faith, her brown eyes wide with hope and examined the toy. "Let me go inside and find a kitchen knife. I may be able to get the tire back on the rim."

He took a couple of steps toward the micro kitchen and retrieved a steak knife. He pushed his laptop back so he could work from the tabletop, and maneuvered the rubber circle onto the plastic rim, fastening the wheels on the doll car. He bent down to her level and handed the toy back to her.

"Thank you." She hugged his neck and ran outside toward her house.

Too stunned to move, Matt stayed in the kneeling position when the door slammed. He'd never been hugged by a child. How could such an insignificant act take away some of his tension? He straightened, rubbed his neck and tried to digest what just happened.

Later in the afternoon, he typed a pivoting scene. A knock infiltrated his fantasy world. He ambled to the door and found Lucinda on the stoop with a covered dish.

"I brought you a serving of flounder and cheese pasta. It's a thank you for fixing Faith's toy." She motioned at her daughter who stood by with all smiles.

"It was nothing." Matt smiled. "Thank you." He sat the plate inside the mini fridge and then grabbed his jacket from the chair. "Want to take a walk?"

"Sure." She stuck her hands in her vest.

They strolled toward the pumpkin patch while Faith skipped ahead.

"I think you have a way with children after all." Lucinda's face brightened.

"I haven't spent much time around little people." He glanced ahead at the Blue Asters with their vivid yellow centers clustered together.

"Faith likes you." Lucinda bent down and picked a flower.

"Can I ask you something?" Matt stopped walking as she gathered the foliage.

"I guess." She put the blossom to her nose and sniffed.

"What brought you to this place in life?"

They both stood and eyed the greenery. Matt noticed her eyebrows lift up. "I don't mean Black Mountain. I'm wondering about you being a single mother."

"Oh." She twisted her mouth and studied his face.

"It's complicated. One minute I was living without responsibilities and before I could adjust to the idea of change, Faith was in my life. I looked at her dimpled cheeks and fell in love. I don't have any regrets. Faith has my heart." She patted her chest.

"What about her father?" Matt spoke quickly. He realized his voice sounded impatient and closed his eyes for a brief second.

"Well." She tossed the flower on the ground. "Like I said, it's complicated. He's not in the picture."

"Are you sorry he's not here to help?"

"I have to face things as they are. Maybe, one day all will be different. Until that time comes, I trust the Lord to guide me." Lucinda took faster steps. "Here's the pumpkin garden." She pointed ahead at the lines of yellow and orange balls that were beginning to resemble a baseball.

"Wow, it's a little more than just a garden. You have a lot of rows."

"Yeah, I sometimes get carried away. Faith loves pumpkins. She likes it when we supply the schools and shelters with the fall treat. We also sell the fruit."

Matt glanced sideways at Lucinda watching her daughter run over to the fruits. "I need to offer an apology. I didn't mean to pry about her father."

"That's fine. No harm done."

"Good." Matt smiled and reached for her hand, surprised that she responded.

Absorbed in the act of holding hands, their eyes locked, Faith's happy glee broke the tenderness between them. He stepped back. "I should get to my novel."

. . ⚘ . .

THE COMPUTER SCREEN went black. He slammed down the lid. Several hours had passed and he'd only written five pages. He walked to the mini fridge, took out a can of cola and moved to the window. Matt turned up the carbonated drink and swallowed a big gulp. His eyes went the distance toward Lucinda's house. Her lights were still on. He recalled their last meeting and laughed at the notion of a single mother afraid to hold hands. Did she really expect him to believe that?

CHAPTER THREE

"Honey, here's your bear." Lucinda handed Faith the stuffed animal and pulled the covers close to her shoulders. "Good night."

"Night-night, Mommy."

Lucinda finished cleaning the kitchen and went into the living room. She walked over to the fireplace, stoked the logs, and sat down in the nearest chair. All evening she mulled over her conversation with Matt. She lowered her head, "Heavenly Father, please guide me. I didn't lie to Matt, but I need Your help." She moved her hair back from her shoulder and pondered questions she couldn't answer. *Faith's father.* She studied the coral polish on her nails. "Lord, I know I need to find out who her father is." She squeezed her hands together. "I love Faith. What if the man takes my child away?"

• • ✦ • •

TWO DAYS LATER, MATT left his desk, and frowned. It was by shear will that he managed to get four chapters written. He rubbed his chin and glared at the computer. *Washington Forever,* the last book in the series would get finished by the deadline. He slapped the table. *Then I'll figure out the rest.*

He stood and grabbed the dish that held Lucinda's thank you meal. Matt pictured her coal black hair that accented big blue eyes and made them sparkle like tropical waters soaking in the summer rays. When she smiled a dimple formed on her right cheek. His fantasy made him inhale with pleasure. How had her life derailed? She was indeed a woman of mystery and his attraction to her was a puzzle.

Matt stepped into the sunshine and stretched. He headed in the direction of Lucinda's house and spotted Faith coming toward him.

"Matt, whatcha doing?" She skipped close and looked up at him.

"I was going to take this container back to your mother."

"Okay." Faith took hold of his finger. "First, let me show you where my doll drove her car."

"Let's not be long." He eyed her as she tugged him toward the pumpkin patch.

They walked past the crop, into the woods beyond. Matt looked back. The tiny house was getting even smaller. "Faith, you shouldn't be going this far from home."

"I like it here." She ran deeper in the woods, toward an overgrown area. "See my playhouse."

Matt followed her to an old wooden arch. Overgrown vines and ferns mangled together to cover broken trees and create a cocoon. He bent down and peered inside the structure. Faith crawled into the circle of foliage and pushed her pink car. "My doll is in the jungle." She thrust the car toward him and giggled.

Matt grabbed the toy. "I think we need to go. Let me help you out of there." He held out his hand for Faith to take, then gave her the toy back. They walked out of the mass of vegetation. "You shouldn't play among those vines. It might be dangerous." He eyed the child. She glanced at him and shrugged. When the tiny house came to view Faith took off running. Her voice trailed behind. "I'll race you home."

Matt stared ahead as the child's pace slowed. She hopped up the step to the back door and skipped past Lucinda.

Seconds later, Matt came to the patio. "I brought your dish. Thanks again for the meal."

"You're quite welcome." Lucinda took the container. "Sit down and take a break from your work." She took a seat in the glider.

Matt sat in the wicker chair opposite Lucinda. "Faith was playing past the pumpkin patch. I encouraged her to come home. Your daughter is a bundle of energy."

"She sure is." A soft laugh filled the distance between them.

Her easy-going nature lightened his mood. He leaned back and relaxed. "I don't know how you do it."

Her face turned serious. "What?"

"Keep up with a child, work, and garden. It seems like a lot."

"Oh." She fanned the air. "I guess its part of being a female. We women juggle many things at once. I have to admit when next fall comes and Faith starts school I'm hoping it gives her energy a new direction. I think she'll enjoy learning different things."

"I remember her telling me she couldn't go because of her birthday." He frowned at the memory.

"Yeah, she turned five a week after school started and they have some rule about that." Lucinda shot a fast gaze toward the sky. "Which reminds me, I need to find her birth certificate."

"Is it missing?" Matt massaged the nape of his neck as he tried to keep up with Lucinda's conversation.

"When we moved here I stashed the tote with diplomas, papers and such in the attic."

"Well, you have some time to look for it." Matt watched her rock the glider as if she was in her own world.

"I do." She turned her attention to him. "How's the book coming?"

"I dislike admitting to a fan that this novel may not be my finest, but I'll make the dead line."

"I'm sure the book will be good. What's next after this one?"

Matt contemplated her questions. Queries he'd pondered before. "All I know is writing. I'll plot another story. But I may take a break first."

"Matt, you mentioned you grew up here. Why did you leave?"

He eyed a white stool. Normally, he changed the subject when someone started a conversation, which made him uncomfortable, but Lucinda didn't strike him as a person who meddled. He gazed at her ocean blues and took a breath. Memories pushed their way forth. "I attended college close by. I was a whiz at inventing any kind of character world. My creative writing professor would give out a picture and asked all the students to write a short story." Matt grinned at the memory. "One of those photographs had me so enthralled I wrote an entire novel. My professor was also an author and had connections. Honestly, it seemed like before I graduated I had an agent. She spoke about Washington. The more we chatted, the bigger my desire to move became."

Matt shook his head. "I told my girlfriend the plans I had to relocate. I even asked her to go with me. She refused. Told me I had a new life waiting."

"That's sad, where is she now?" Lucinda pressed her lips tight.

"This was around the time that my parents were in the process of moving. I came back to help load the furniture hauler. Sonya was gone." Matt leaned his elbows on his legs. "Some months later, I received a letter from her with no return address. All it said was that she was dying. When I got a break from my book tour I came back to find her and the house she'd lived in had been sold. The new owner said the realtor told them she was deceased."

"Goodness." Lucinda put her hand to her mouth. "I'm sorry. I know that was hard."

"Yes. I've often wondered if it would've been different had I stayed in town."

"Matt, things happen that we can't explain. Sometimes it's better not to torture ourselves over the 'what ifs.' You did the best you could at the time. You had no control over the rest."

He looked her way and let out a breath. "I suppose."

"Hey." She tilted her head and grinned. "I promised Faith homemade ice cream after dinner tonight. Come join us. It's going to be chocolate."

"How can I say no to that?" He got to his feet. "I better go and get to typing."

"I'll see you about seven."

"Okay." He strolled down the steps.

. . ❧ . .

A CHILD'S GIGGLES FLOWED from within. Matt knocked hard on the back door to make his presence known. Seconds later Faith let him in.

"Mommy says you're eating ice cream with us."

"I am. Is that okay with you?"

The child put her hand on her chin and stretched her neck to look up, "As long as you don't eat it all."

Lucinda entered the room as she spoke. "Faith, use your manners. Matt is a guest. Get the napkins while I put the bowls out." She nibbled at her lip. "Sorry about that. Kids usually say what's on their minds."

"It's fine." He nodded. "If I were her I wouldn't want all the chocolate eaten either."

Matt sat at the end of the table and waited while Lucinda scooped the dessert. She handed Faith the first dish of the cold treat, gave Matt a full bowl and then took the seat next to him. "Let's be thankful before we eat." She glanced at Matt and then bowed. "Heavenly Father, bless this ice cream and help us to walk with you each day. Amen."

Matt almost repeated her affirmation. He scooped a spoon of chocolate and wondered why the Amen wanted to topple from his tongue so easy. He hadn't been around anyone who thanked God since his last visit to his parents' house. He scanned the table at the mother and daughter enjoying their ice cream. "This is good." He spooned more of the dessert.

"Thanks. It's not much to it. All I do is add ingredients and freeze."

"I'm enjoying it and I think Faith is too." He looked at the little girl. She nodded while foraging in her bowl for the last bite.

A half hour later, Matt watched his surroundings. Lucinda placed the rest of the ice cream in the freezer. "Honey," She touched the little girl's hair. "Go in the living room and watch a cartoon. You can finish the movie about your favorite princess."

Matt glanced at the child as she trotted off. "She's a good girl." He paused, surprised that he commented about the child. "You're a great mother."

"Thanks, I try." She began to load the dishwasher. "Faith is a fairly well-behaved child. I'm lucky."

Matt stood and gave Lucinda the bowls. He moved closer to give her the last dish and stopped short when she turned and stepped into his arms. He froze and stared into the gaze that met him. He was lost, drowned in a pool of clear blue, to a place where nothing mattered. He muttered. "I hope you don't mind." His arms circled her, as his mouth tenderly found hers.

Matt's heart beat to the tune of a new awareness as soft lips responded to his caress. He tasted her kiss and realized he was attracted to her in ways he'd never been to any woman before. He continued to hold her in his arms. "You're a unique woman Lucinda. I hope you don't regret kissing me."

"No." She licked her lips.

Matt felt her move away. He followed her gaze and noticed Faith standing beside them. "I'll go. We'll talk later."

He slipped outside and ambled to his abode, mentally replaying the last few seconds before the child interrupted them.

· · ❧ · ·

THE NEXT NIGHT LUCINDA pulled Faith's bedroom door partly closed. She stepped into the hallway, leaned against the wall and touched her lips. Matt's kiss still played in her imagination. If she concentrated, she could conjure up the warmth of his arms around her. She huffed, not willing to admit that she wanted more of his touch.

Lucinda changed into lounge clothes, grabbed her laptop and completed a customer profile for a new financial account.

When she finished the forms, she moved the cursor to her favorites and clicked on several recipes she hoped to try with this year's pumpkin crop. She eyed a picture of a Pumpkin Soufflé as a pop up from a bookstore she'd recently visited covered part of the page and flashed the latest book from a suspense trilogy. Again, her mind wandered to Matt and how wonderful his breath felt as it lightly brushed against her cheek. She laid a hand on her chest and felt the beat of her heart. A reminder of how it raced as his arms cradled her. The guy was certainly handsome. His brown eyes could pierce a soul. Matt was also fun to talk to, but he would only be here for a short time. Any idea of having a relationship with him had to be dispelled. Faith was her commitment and one that she loved without regrets.

Another advertisement flashed across the lap top screen. The side bar highlighted a black and white picture from the eighteen hundreds and listed a website designed to track down past relatives. She reminisced about her parents who'd passed away years before Faith was born and recalled the day they moved to North Carolina.

Faith. She'd been a beautiful baby with chubby little cheeks and silky fine hair. Lucinda lay back on the pillow. She owed it to the child to find answers. One day she might ask questions. Tomorrow, she'd find the birth records.

DUST FLOATED THROUGH the stale air of the attic space. Lucinda blew at a strand of hair hanging from her barrette and lifted a boot box with "Faith's stuff" written on top. She rearranged it and carefully made her way down the narrow steps. At the bottom of the stairs, she spied Faith going into the kitchen. "What do you need honey?"

"I want a cookie."

"Well," Lucinda followed the child and glanced at the time. "I guess it will be okay. Only one." She handed Faith an oatmeal cookie.

"Mommy what's in the box?" Faith took hold of the treat and dropped her teddy bear.

"Some of your baby things. I thought I'd see if I can find your birth certificate. You'll need it for school."

"What's a birth certify?" Faith bit into the cookie.

"Certificate." Lucinda corrected. "It's an official paper that shows where and when you were born."

"Mommy, where was I born?"

"In New York. That's where we lived before we moved here." Lucinda sat at the table and opened the lid. She removed a faded onesie. The white bodysuit with pink hearts looked smaller than she remembered. She grinned and turned toward Faith. "This was your first outfit."

"It's funny with those snaps all over." Faith fingered the material.

"They make it easier to get diapers off." Lucinda reached into the box again. "Here is your first pair of booties." She laid the cloth shoes on the table.

"Mommy." Faith pulled the tie string. "These won't keep your feet dry in the rain."

"You were too little to walk. I had to carry you." Lucinda commented while she unhooked the manila envelope that held her important papers pertaining to Faith, and the original birth certificate. "You recall seeing your Sunday school teacher with her little boy. It takes a while before babies can walk."

"Ms. Green's baby cries a lot." Faith stood. "Can I have another cookie?"

"No. Please, go play. We'll have lunch soon." Lucinda laid the certificate out as Faith gathered her bear from the floor and wandered into the next room.

The baby items brought back so many memories. She found it hard to recall the six-pound infant that she'd loved from the first touch of her little fingers. She picked up a cloth shoe and ran her finger over the pink bow. Never had she regretted her decision to keep Faith. Not that she'd considered any other choices. She grinned and arranged the infant wear back in its resting place. "Lord, thank you for looking out after us and for drawing me to your salvation. Perhaps, one day you'll make a way for me to have love, and for Faith to have a father."

She unfolded the birth document and pondered how much her life had changed in five years. She'd become a mother and a Christian, trusting in Jesus.

Lucinda focused on the hospital record, skimmed over the section that held the mother's information, to the line that listed the father. She wheezed, grabbed her throat and coughed when the bold type leaped out at her. The paper fell to the floor. "Goodness, No!"

A few deep breaths later, she bent down, shaking, she scooped up the certificate and studied the writing across the page. *Why didn't she confide in me?* She looked toward the ceiling and shook her head. "I would have made other choices, I think."

Lucinda stuffed the document back in the box and placed everything on a shelf over the cabinet. *I need to find out more.* She rubbed her temple. Why hadn't she paid attention to the birth certificate sooner? "Jesus, I messed up."

The cell phone chimed. Absentmindedly, she noted her friend's number. "Hello."

"Hi, can you give me some advice?"

"Cynthia, sometimes I don't think I'm capable of adding my two-cents to anything."

"Why do you say that? You're one of the most levelheaded women I know."

"Maybe now, but I haven't always been." Lucinda sat down and rubbed her head. "What's up?"

She half-heartily listened to a birthday dilemma about what gift her friend should get her mother-in-law.

"I remember you mentioning that she collects crystal bells. Get her a bell from another country. Her birthday is a month away." Lucinda pushed her chair up against the table. "You know the ones she has. Go online and find something unique."

"Lucinda, that's a great idea. Thanks."

"Not a problem. I'm glad you called. I need you to stand in agreement with me in prayer about something."

"You know I will. What is it?"

"Years ago, I made a blunder." Lucinda swallowed hard. "I don't want to mess up again. I need God to smooth over any troubles that might come back to haunt me."

"You're scaring me. What is it?"

"I can't talk about it right now, just pray with me that the Lord will lead me to set the past straight and my heart won't get broken."

"I will. Lucinda, remember that verse in Psalm 91:14. It says, He will deliver you because you know His name and love him."

"Thanks"

She ended the conversation as the verse from Matthew 7:7 came to mind, "*Ask, and it will be given to you; seek, and you will find; knock, and it will be opened to you.*" She understood that the Lord meant to knock for His salvation, but she also hoped it meant to seek His help in situations. She bowed her head. "Lord, I've made mistakes in my life. All I want is what's right for Faith, and her father. "Please, Heavenly Father, guide me."

CHAPTER FOUR

Matt shook his head at the nonsense he'd typed and hit delete. He knew better than to write those kinds of fillers. Even a novice writer wouldn't do that. He saved his file, strolled to the refrigerator and grabbed a bottle of water.

Outside on the miniscule porch he searched the horizon. Matt shaded his eyes from the fall sunshine and examined the outlying field. He debated about the green stems of the pumpkin plants. To him it appeared that the ground was decorated with orange. The only thing he knew about pumpkins was a little he'd researched years ago for a scene in one of his books. The information certainly wasn't enough to understand how long it would take for the baseball size fruit to grow into maturity. While he viewed the acreage, a child's vigorous laugh made him turn his head toward the drive that led to his renter's house. *Faith. Were all children that active?* His mind went to Lucinda as quick as the breeze that whooshed through his hair. He took a sip of water and dabbed the wetness from his mouth with the back of his hand. Her kiss had made him feel like a teen again.

As if he'd called up Lucinda, he noticed her walking toward him. He smiled when she got closer distance.

"Hi. It's a nice day, isn't it?"

"Very nice." Lucinda glanced around at the fall foliage. "I was wondering if you would join Faith and me for dinner.

Nothing fancy, hot dogs and fries. Faith's favorite." She grinned and looked intently at Matt. When she felt her face flush, she turned away for a second.

"It happens to be a favorite of mine too. Takes me back to college days when I used to grab a couple dogs from the local deli before I hit the books." His face lit with happiness from the memory.

"Good, I'll see you about six."

Matt saw her turn to leave. He rushed to her side. "I hope you understand that I wasn't being disrespectful when I kissed you."

"I hadn't thought you impolite." She sighed and added. "I would be lying if I said I didn't enjoy it, but as I've mentioned, my life is complicated. You're only here until Thanksgiving then you'll be going back to Washington."

Matt walked closer. "Maybe, we can just enjoy the attraction between us." He lightly captured her mouth with his.

Time stopped. He basked in the softness of her lips. The mixture of peppermint and lilac intrigued his senses as their kiss deepened. He felt her hands glide along his back. They were lost in a pool of togetherness.

She moved away. "I'll see you at dinner."

Matt gazed after her as she hurried down the path toward her house. He licked his lips, went back inside and took a seat in front of his laptop, fueled with ammunition to place his character in the arms of her nemesis.

. . ❧ . .

THE CRICKETS PLAYED a melody as Matt strolled toward Lucinda's place. He took a deep breath and inhaled the country air. It wasn't vehicle exhaust and dirty city street fumes that traveled to his senses. It was a clean crispness. The fragrance reminded him of a fresh apple mixed with honeysuckle. He angled his head and eyed the sky. Five years in the city had made him oblivious to the twinkling stars and the beauty, which surrounded him. He stopped, absorbed in the tapestry of the atmosphere. Again, he debated his decision to move from his small town, to the hustle of an overpopulated city. "Was it too much cluttering, clouding my mind?"

He picked up his pace. The light from the back deck of Lucinda's house paved a path for him to see her sweeping a step. It was a simple act but the way she swayed as she pushed the broom drew attention, even clad in jeans he could make out the outline of her well-toned legs.

"You okay?" She stood the broom against the siding. "I noticed you standing in the shadows."

"I was admiring the stars. Living in the heart of Washington with all the street lights has made me forget how majestic the sky can be."

"For sure." She glimpsed toward heaven. "God did a wonderful job creating the universe."

"Mom always says that we can't behold all the beauty God has in store for us." Matt shifted his weight. *Where had that come from?*

Lucinda grinned. "I didn't know you were a believer."

"I used to go to church with Mom and Dad. I haven't forgotten my religious upbringing. It seems when I moved away I became too busy for worship."

"Life gets hectic. It's easy to let things get out of hand. Still, it's important to remember who Jesus is and what He gave up for us." She opened the storm door. "Redemption and God's words also keep our days on track."

"I know you're right." Matt followed her into the kitchen. "You accepted Christ into your heart after moving here?"

"Yes, Faith caught a cold, and off to the clinic we went. While I was waiting, the lady next to me introduced herself and encouraged me to visit her church." She shrugged. "A week later, I decided to visit Believers' House of Prayer. God dealt with my heart. Not long after that, I accepted His call. And Cynthia, the woman at the doctor's office has been my best friend ever since." Her eyes shined as she spoke. "Have a seat." She pointed to a chair. "I'll get you a glass of tea. We can chat while I set the table." She placed the ketchup down. "My invitation for you to join us at church is ongoing."

"Thanks." He accepted the beverage. "I may take you up on the offer. I do need to redirect my life a little. Reading Ecclesiastes gave me a few ideas about my work in progress." He sipped his tea. "The verses mention a time to..." His eyes grew wider. "They've given me some thoughts for a plot."

"Good." Lucinda placed the buns and condiments on the table. "The reason I like your books is because you don't use bad language or create overly suggestive intimate scenes. I read mostly Christian authors' works now. Your novels are the only secular ones that I still enjoy."

"I appreciate that. I guess I write clean plots because of the way I was raised. That and my mother would have my hide if I wrote any other way." He laughed.

Lucinda giggled. "I never figured you for a Mommy's boy."

"I'm not, but I'm smart enough to remember that it's best to err on the side of caution."

"Touché." Lucinda grinned. "Let me get Faith washed for dinner. I'll be right back."

The clicking of the wall clock drew Matt's attention to the round dial. Each number had a different flower on it. He glanced around the eat-in kitchen. Over the door was a wooden plaque with, "God shed His Grace on Thee." He remembered a Bible study with the same title. He tried to bring to mind the children's class as Lucinda entered with Faith.

"Matt!" Faith hurled to his side and hugged him."

"Hi." He eyed the child, still not accustomed to the easy way she greeted him. "So, you like hotdogs?"

"Yeah." Her little head bobbed up and down as she scooted in her seat. "My bestest meal."

"Best." He laughed and watched Lucinda place the weenies on the table.

"Matt, since you're familiar with our Lord will you say a blessing?"

He wrinkled his forehead. "I can."

He looked across the table. Lucinda and Faith had their heads bowed. His lips turned up. He figured Lucinda was challenging him. True, he hadn't asked the Lord for anything in five years, but like putting on a comfortable glove, he spoke. "Heavenly Father, thank you for our bounty. We ask you to bless our daily endeavors and to sanctify this meal. Amen"

"Amen." Lucinda quickly added.

"You should come with us to church. You say a pretty prayer." Faith's mouth turned up and made her eyes crinkle.

"Maybe some time." He nodded and paid attention as Faith enthusiastically bit into her hotdog.

As they chatted, the child worked on her loaded frankfurter like it was an expensive gourmet meal.

"It's a wonder she isn't big for her age." He lifted his lip at the request for another helping of fries, noting Lucinda only forked out a small offering.

"I'll take a few more." He held out his plate.

"Mommy makes the bestest fries ever!" Faith chimed in as she swiped her potato in ketchup.

"She is a good cook." Matt glanced at Lucinda.

"Thank you." Her eyes met his for a brief second before she turned her attention back to her daughter.

The rest of the meal was savored with light chatter. Faith tried to dominate the conversation with tidbits about her gerbil's adventures in its roller ball. Lucinda noticed Faith had finished eating.

"Honey, why don't you go feed your pet?"

"Okay." She slid off her chair and hurried to the next room.

"She sure is energetic." Matt got to his feet and helped Lucinda put away the mustard and leftovers.

"No more than any other five year old. Would you like some banana pudding? I didn't tell Faith I made any because it's too late for her to have sugar. She'll enjoy some tomorrow."

"Sounds good."

"I'll get the dessert bowls." She cleared the rest of the table.

He scooted the chair back and waited for Lucinda before he sampled the treat. "This is good."

"It's a recipe that came from my mother."

"Where are you parents?" He savored the creamy filling letting it satisfy his taste buds.

"They passed away about eight years ago. Mother had a bad case of flu. That year she was one of the statistics. It was hard. Dad's history of high blood pressure took its toll on him a couple years later."

"I'm sorry. I know that must have been hard."

"It was." She took the last bite of pudding. "Can I ask you something personal?"

"I suppose..." He hesitated and scraped his bottom lip with his teeth.

"You mentioned a girlfriend here. Who was she and does she have family close?"

"No family. Why?" Matt creased his brow.

"Perhaps, I'm curious about the lady in my favorite author's past." She grinned and put her hair behind her ear in a flirty move.

"Sonya McCray was her name. She lived on Mason Street. What about your first love?"

"Not much to say. Like you I was just out of college. He was my employer and a big mistake." She lightly tapped the table top with her nail." I found out he was a married piece of scum."

"Wow." He straightened in his seat and studied Lucinda. "That's tough."

"Well, he was. Any married man that lies and cheats, must be lowlife."

"I agree with you, it's not good." He put up his hand, "So, Faith's father?"

"Let's change the subject." She rose from her seat.

"Sure." He stood. "Our past is gone. We both should concentrate on the now." He stood, put his arms around her and lowered his mouth toward hers. A giggle flowed into the room and interrupted what he was sure was destined to be.

"It's getting past Faith's bedtime." She touched Matt's hand and turned toward the back door. "We should say good night."

"Okay. He brushed her cheek with a kiss and left.

· · ❧ · ·

LUCINDA SETTLED FAITH down for the night and went to her quarters to prepare for bed. After a quick shower, she leaned against her pillow and flipped the pages in her Bible, looking for scriptures that would give her strength. Automatically, she went to Philippians, chapter four. "God, I know I can face anything with the strength your word provides. I believe a difficult path waits. Please, lead me, In Jesus name, Amen."

She reviewed several passages and then found her way to the book of Joshua before she closed her Bible and snuggled into the pillow. Restlessness had her turning from side to side. In the darkness of night, she quoted part of the scripture, "Do not be frightened, and do not be dismayed, for the LORD your God is with you wherever you go." She squeezed her eyes tighter imagining what lay ahead. "Give me the wisdom and the fortitude to do the right thing."

CHAPTER FIVE

Matt was glad he'd left the outside light on. With that, and the glow from Lucinda's lamppost, finding the way in the dark was easy. He glanced at his wristwatch and realized he'd been sitting in the lounge chair in front of his tiny house for forty-five minutes, absorbed in the twinkling stars. The glitters seemed to be some kind of Morse code that only the heavens knew. He stood, stretched and went inside.

Matt turned on his laptop with the idea of moving forward in his make-believe world. He pulled up a site to research and then began to type a scene where his character walked into a darkened alley. The vision of a damp, cold garbage filled backstreet was disturbed with his recent dinner jaunt. He stopped typing and tried to put pieces together of Lucinda just out of college. It offered him some answers. She must have been manipulated. Faith's father had to be married and didn't want anyone to know about the child.

. . ⚘ . .

THE NEXT MORNING MATT walked the small space and exhaled. "Man!" He fought to recall the idea that came to him in the night. It was a perfect way to steer his character into the pivoting chapter that he needed. "Why didn't I get out of bed and write it down?" He sat back down at his computer and clicked his favorites to search the link that he'd read the night before. It had to hold the clue he needed. As he skimmed the columns he came to the Bible web site he'd marked the day Lucinda's scripture plagued his curiosity.

He clicked the page. A pastel-colored header announced, "Bible Wisdom." He glanced at the bold caption. The title pronounced, 1 Corinthians 1:18 "For the preaching of the cross is to them that perish foolishness; but unto us which are saved it is the power of God."

He scrutinized the verse and continued to read several paragraphs. Before he left the Internet search, he visited one of the writer's sites and spied the forum. Christian fiction seemed to be the topic of the day. He reared back in his chair and read the tête-à-tête. The faith-filled writers commented about their craft being a part of them, a ministry first, anything else second. He exited the screen when a memory surfaced. Years ago in New York at a conference, he met a famous Christian author. What amazed him was that the man had stayed on the best-selling list the longest of any author, even him with his secular stories.

Matt rose from his seat and pushed the front door back to step outside. A chill revealed itself in the air as his mind lingered on fiction genres. His books weren't X-rated but they did have gore. People seemed to enjoy the violence weaved in the pages. He put his arm over his head and stretched with a realization. He'd always created stories that readers responded to but he'd never written a novel that stemmed from a belief deep within his heart. Bits from a verse he'd read earlier passed in his mind. *Unto us which are saved it is the power of God.* A breeze circled around him. *Is that how believers wrote?*

Hurried footsteps broke his meditation. He turned his head as Lucinda approach.

"Have you seen Faith? She told me she was going to the back yard to swing. I can't find her." Lucinda's voice broke in syllables.

"No, I haven't," Lucinda's brow wrinkle from worry.

"Here." He pointed to the fold out lounger he'd placed outside.

"I have to go through the pumpkin patch and find her. She loves running in between the fruit."

"You sit." He gently steered her into the chair. "I'll look for her. You're too upset to do any good." He started to walk and glanced back. "I'll return with Faith."

His feet made haste toward the field of growing pumpkins. He walked the rows and searched for the child. *Nothing.*

Matt was about to head back to his tiny house when he remembered the child's hiding place. Picking up his pace he made the way through the thicket where the undergrowth made a perfect fort for a little girl. As he closed in on a tangled creeper plant, a cry sounded. The sobs made him scurry over the brush.

"Faith, are you all right?" Matt bent down and took a gander into the opening.

"I..." Faith sniffled, "Hurt." She wiped tears from her cheeks.

"What happened?" He scooted closer.

"I got hung in a vine and fell. Now my foot hurts. I can't move it much." Faith held her ankle and whimpered.

"Here take my hand. I'll help." He got on his knees and tried to crawl into the opening.

"It's too sore." She shook her head.

"Faith, I can't get closer. Princess, you have to come to me. I'll take you home to Mommy."

"No." Her voice rose and she squeezed her eyes shut.

"Honey." He scratched his head and debated ways to get the child's cooperation. "What can I do to get you to be brave and scoot nearer?"

Matt pressed his lips tight. He knew nothing about children. His mind reeled with indecision. He glanced at her foot. The swelling told him that she probably had a sprain.

"Maybe." Faith hesitated and rubbed her ankle. "You could go to church with me Sunday and help me get to class."

His head jerked away from the child's foot to her face. His fingers cradled his neck. *Church.* "You can go another time."

"No I can't." Her high pitched tone nasally. "I have to go."

He put his hand up in defeat and changed the tone of his voice so he wouldn't scare her. "Why is this Sunday important?"

"I'm working on a project. It's something special for Mommy." She started to whimper once more.

"Okay." He stared at the umber-brown ground veiled with twigs. "If you be brave and crawl to me. I'll take you home."

"You'll go with me to church and help me get to Sunday school?"

"Yes. He paused and looked at Faith's wide eyes full of expectation. "I'll take you to class. Come to me." He extended his hand.

"You have to promise." Faith moved her good leg.

"I promise." He nodded with approval while Faith crawled on one knee dragging her injured foot. "That's right, only a few more paces."

Matt scooped her up in his arms, crawled the few feet in a crab like position until he could stand. His shirt was wet from Faith's tears but her cries had turned into hiccups. He cuddled her in his arms and picked up his pace toward Lucinda.

He got closer to the tiny house and saw Lucinda stand and run toward him.

"Oh, Goodness. Thank you Jesus!" Lucinda grabbed Faith and smiled at Matt. "I appreciate you finding her." She turned sideways and hugged him with her free arm.

"Mommy, I hurt."

"Honey, let's get you home."

"Lucinda, you may need to go to the Urgent Care Center." He leaned next to her and whispered. "Faith's ankle is swollen badly. It might be a sprain."

"Oh dear." She examined the child's foot. "We'll go right away."

"Do you need assistance?" He laid his hand on her shoulder.

"No, we'll be fine, but here." She gave him her cell phone. "Put your number in and I'll let you know what the doctor says."

"Keep me posted." He returned her phone.

"I will."

• • ❧ • •

LUCINDA'S CELL VIBRATED. She glanced at her friend's number while Faith sat on her lap and scrummed. "It won't be long honey. Try to relax."

"Hi Cynthia."

"Where are you? I stopped by your house to drop off the records for Audi's store. My uncle will never learn how to use a computer."

"Faith went into the woods and fell. Her ankle is bruised. We're at the clinic."

"Oh-no. I hope it's not too bad."

"I'll let you know after we see the doctor and I'll get those tax papers later."

"Of course. I'll send up a prayer for Faith."

"Thanks."

As she ended the call, her notions strayed from Faith's injury to the handsome author who temporarily lived on her property. The picture of Matt cradling Faith in his arms as he carried her would forever play in her mind. The man was certainly a puzzle. One minute he acted like he didn't want to be around anyone and the next second he was offering his support.

"Faith Wise." The nurse's announcement pushed Lucinda's thoughts aside. She carried Faith and followed the assistant.

"Tell me what happened." The nurse studied Faith's foot and wrote on her clipboard as Lucinda spoke.

"She was supposed to be playing on her swing." She looked at her daughter, then back at the nurse. "But instead she went into the woods. Faith tells me she tripped and fell."

"Can you tell me what happened sweetie?" The nurse coaxed Faith to lie down.

"I tripped on some weeds. My foot twisted under me."

"We'll have the doctor look at your sprain." The assistant nodded at Lucinda and closed the examination room's door.

Four hours later, Lucinda leaned the child-size crutches against the wall and propped Faith's foot up on a pillow as she tucked her in bed. "You've had a long evening."

"Mommy, I'm tired."

"That's because the doctor gave you something to help you rest." Lucinda kissed Faith on the cheek.

"Will you make me a meatloaf for after Sunday school tomorrow?"

"I can, but I don't think we'll make church this Sunday."

"Pleassse..." Faith stretched the word. "I need to go."

Lucinda glanced at Faith. A tear slid down the little girl's cheek. "If you feel that strong about church, I'll get you there, somehow."

"Thanks Mommy. Don't worry, I have help."

"Of course you do." Lucinda grinned at Faith." Let's say a prayer before you fall asleep."

. . ⌘ . .

TIME PASSED. MATT RELAXED in his jogging pants. He'd managed to get more pages written, but his normal struggles with his writing were escalated by Faith's accident. He recalled the way the child snuggled close when he carried her to the safety of her mother's arms. The silence throughout the small quarters ended when his phone sang out a tune. He noticed Lucinda's name on the screen.

"Hi, I was getting concerned."

"They x-rayed Faith's ankle. She has a fracture. The doctor says it's small, but she has to wear a cast for six weeks. And can you believe she insists on going to church and even asked for meatloaf." She laughed.

"It's going to be hard to keep her settled down for six weeks. She's an active child."

"Yes, but I think the weight of the cast will slow her for a while."

"I was writing and Faith's accident kept tugging at me. It's amazing how in an instant things can change."

"Turn on a dime, that's what a friend use to say. It certainly doesn't take much for life to head down another path." Lucinda took off her flats, "How about you?"

"What?" Matt paused before responding. "Sorry, I don't understand the question."

"I was thinking about adjustments we have to make in life. How does the big time author take change?"

"Haven't had many. I guess I've been lucky."

"Or it hasn't been your season." Lucinda stifled a yawn.

"Seasons. You're talking about those Bible passages." Matt climbed the steps to the loft as they chatted.

"You know we all have different times when things happen." Lucinda's voice mellowed.

"Suppose so. It could be that I'm getting ready to find out."

"Why do you say that?" She questioned.

"I think I'm hitting that seven-year itch as they say, with my writing."

"Seven? I don't understand. I've only been reading your books for five."

"I actually started when I was in college. I have a few electronic books published by a small press. I didn't find my agent until later." He stretched his leg.

"Matt, why do you think your books will change?"

"I've realized that all these years I've been scribing subjects that were expected of me. I may try something different when this book is finished."

"If you feel that way, then you should. The fans who read your books will understand. I do."

"Thank you. You'll be the first to know when I switch genres."

"There's something you should know." Lucinda's voice floated across the airwaves slowly.

"What is it?"

"Sonya, your old sweetheart was a good friend of mine."

"What, how?"

"She came to New York. We met at a deli. I offered to show her around. We were almost inseparable for a while."

"Then you knew she was sick?" He ran his hand through his hair and purposely lowered his voice to keep his irritation at bay. "Why didn't you mention it earlier?"

"I didn't know if I should."

"Lucinda, please." His words broke with an uneven breath. "Will you tell me what happened?"

"The reason Sonya came to New York was to see a specialist." Her tone softened. "There was nothing the doctors could do. She sublet the apartment next to mine but the last month she lived she stayed in the hospital. I spent as much time as possible with her those last two months. That's why I moved to Black Mountain. Sonya talked so much about this town."

He let go of his resolve and snapped, "I can't believe you didn't tell me this sooner!"

"I'm sorry. Some things from my life aren't easy to speak about. I like to go to the Lord in prayer before I confide in people."

"I guess I understand." He noticed indecisiveness in her words. "You don't have to be afraid to unburden your heart to me." He took a deep breath and chuckled to ease the situation. "I promise not to put it in a book."

"That's a relief." Lucinda laughed. "I have something else I need to talk to you about, but like I said. I want to pray about it." She yawned. "I'd better get some rest."

"Okay. Have a good night. And when you pray God will tell you that I'm a trustworthy listener."

"He will?" She smiled, despite the fact that the secret she needed to reveal would without doubt be a thorn between them.

CHAPTER SIX

Darkness circled her. Normally, Lucinda relaxed in the rejuvenation of the nighttime, but tonight the silence of her room made her squirm. She tossed in bed unsure of her place in life. Her whispered prayer broke the silence in the room. "Heavenly Father, I love Faith. I don't want things to change. Amen." She balled up her pillow. A Bible verse came to her remembrance. "Let us draw near with a sincere heart in full assurance of faith, having our hearts sprinkled clean from an evil conscience and our bodies washed with pure water." She repositioned her head. *Hebrews. Jesus, I know what you're saying. I need to have faith and do the right thing.* "Lord, give me a sign."

$$\cdot\cdot\,\infty\,\cdot\cdot$$

THE NEXT MORNING LUCINDA took Faith's favorite meal out of the oven. The warmth from the range helped soothe her chill. The weather had nothing to do with her shivers. Inevitable change loomed. As she placed the dish on the counter, a yell flowed into the room.

"Mommy, help me."

"I'm coming." Lucinda jogged down the hallway to her child's room.

"I can't get my dress on but my ankle doesn't hurt too bad." Faith touched her cast.

"Badly." Lucinda corrected. "Let's get dressed. We'll eat some cereal before we go."

"Okay, Mommy. I want to wear my purple skirt."

A half-hour later, Lucinda grinned at Faith as she scooped the last of her cinnamon squares, and announced she was ready.

"Okay, let me get your coat and help you to the car. We have to be careful because you're still learning how to use crutches."

"No." Lucinda eyed Faith.

"Mommy, I already have some help."

"I'll be right back." She shook her head at Faith's insistence that somehow she could do it on her own.

Lucinda made her way to the kitchen with two coats. She was assisting Faith with her jacket when a knock sounded.

"There's Matt." Faith pulled the cuff of her sleeve.

"What?" She questioned the child while she opened the door. "Hello."

"Morning Lucinda." Matt nodded at Faith. "How's the princess?"

"I'm better, I think." Faith giggled.

"I promised this little one I'd help her to Sunday school."

"Matt." Faith groaned, and put her finger on her lips. "Shh."

"Not a word." He made a twisting motion close to his mouth with his fingers.

"I don't understand." Lucinda looked at Matt in his Khakis' and button up shirt, instead of his usual writing attire of jeans and a sweatshirt. She turned her attention to Faith. Her brow knitted together.

"Your daughter has something important to do. I promised to see that she made it to church."

"Oh, so that's why she kept telling me that she had help." Lucinda started to put on her coat.

"I guess." Matt rushed to aid Lucinda with her fall covering which matched the lavender stripes in her gray and black knee length dress. His hands lingered on her shoulders. He leaned close and whispered in her ear. "You look beautiful." Matt stepped back and glanced sideways at the child. "I'll carry Faith to the car."

Lucinda retrieved the crutches and followed Matt outside to quickly open the back door while he buckled the child's seatbelt.

In the few miles, Faith chatted to Matt about her gerbil sleeping in her room so she could watch him play on his wheel. Lucinda pulled into the parking lot of the church and turned off the engine.

"We're here." She tossed the keys in her oversized purse. "Faith will need to stay with us until they dismiss for children's service."

"Not a problem." Matt cast an eye over the front of the church. "I'll get her out of the car and take her inside and then we can assist her, while she maneuvers her crutches."

"Thanks." Lucinda grabbed her Bible.

She walked beside Matt and nodded at an older man. His starched white shirt stood out in contrast to his burgundy-cuffed slacks. "Pastor Lamoure, this is Matt Blake."

"Welcome son." The older gentleman greeted Matt. "Hello." He touched Faith's hand. "Little lady, Cynthia told me that you had a bad fall."

"I have a cast." She moved her leg to draw his attention to the orange mold.

"I see. It's good you have a helper." The church leader grinned at Matt. "Are you visiting?"

"I'm renting Lucinda's tiny house for a while. I grew up here. I'm Walter and Debbie Blake's son."

"Yes. I think they moved right after I took over for the senior pastor. I hope they're enjoying retirement?"

"Mom says each day is a blessing."

"Good for them." Pastor Lamoure looked ahead at the additional people approaching. "It's nice to have you with us this morning."

"Come on, let's get Faith settled." Lucinda smiled as they stepped forward toward the main worship section. She noticed a woman rush down the aisle toward them and let out a gasp. *Joan Burr.* She glanced sideways at Matt wanting to warn him. Before she could speak, Joan glided up next to them.

"Lucinda. Who's this nice looking gentleman escorting you today?"

"Joan, this is Matt Blake." She glanced his way. "Matt, meet Joan Burr."

"Well, hello." The woman tilted her head, smiled and extended her hand, complete with a rosebud color manicure to match her eye shadow.

"It's nice to meet you." Matt returned the welcome.

"I haven't seen you around town." Joan touched Matt's arm.

"I'm here on vacation, but Black Mountain is my hometown."

"Certainly haven't noticed you bringing a man to church before." Joan addressed Lucinda as if Matt wasn't there.

"No, I guess not." She gave Matt a sideways glance as Joan's husband approached.

"Dear." He put his arm around Joan. "We should get a seat. It's nice to see a visitor today." He reached out and shook hands with Matt. "I'm Clifford Burr."

"Matt Blake. I'm sure I'll enjoy the service."

"Do excuse us." Lucinda touched Matt's arm and steered him to the other side of the room. "Sorry about that. Joan is a unique lady."

"Unique." He smiled. "Lucinda, I'm the writer. I know unique is used to describe good or bad. That woman is nosey."

"You're right." She leaned closer to Matt. "She always searches out the latest happenings about everyone in town." Her grin widened when Matt shook his head in understanding.

"Her husband must have the patience of Job as they say." He glanced around the room.

After the morning's prayer, a couple of songs from the choir and congregation, the exhorter announced children's service.

They stood and Lucinda lowered her voice. "I'll show you where Faith's preschool is."

"I'll walk behind and make sure her steps are stable with those crutches."

While they ambled to the other side of the room, they stopped several times for Lucinda to introduce Matt and recount Faith's accident. She finally made their way to a hallway, where rooms lined each side. The third door on the right stood open. A woman the same age of Matt turned. Her eyes shined. Happiness lined her mouth.

"Hi." Lucinda greeted her friend. "Cynthia, this is Matt Blake."

"Mr. Blake. It's wonderful to meet you. I like your books." She paused. "But I have to admit that I skip chapters. I hope you'll sign one for me."

"Please, call me Matt. May I ask why you skip chapters?"

"I enjoyed the story line, but I dislike a lot of violence." She slightly grinned and looked toward Lucinda. "Faith will be ready after church." Cynthia helped the child to her desk.

In the main worship center, Lucinda and Matt took their place in the middle pew. She looked briefly at him as Pastor Lamoure addressed the congregation.

"Friends, this is a wonderful day in the Lord." He paused and smiled. "As with any day there's never certainty in our lives. We wake and know not what path we'll end up on. We can certainly be assured that life always changes." He looked down at his Bible. "Maybe, it's a small alteration. The café was out of your favorite brand of coffee. Perhaps your day turned into a challenge because you're involved in a little accident on the way to work. No matter, change is inevitable."

The leader of the church lifted his Holy Book and stepped to the side of the podium. "It's natural to get anxious. Nevertheless, God has a plan. He wants good things for His children. We must put aside our apprehension and trust in Him with faithfulness. Let's turn in our Bibles to the book of Joshua. Joshua proved he had strong faith because he followed orders that God gave him, despite the way things looked."

Pastor Lamoure highlighted the struggles, which shadowed Joshua, and his mighty victory. He glanced at the congregation. "It was because of his obedience and faith. In

Joshua 1:9 we read, 'Have not I commanded thee? Be strong and of a good courage; be not afraid, neither be thou dismayed: for the LORD thy God is with thee whithersoever thou goest.' That, ladies and gentleman, sums it up. God is with us. We have His word for our guidance. If we stand firm, we overcome in Jesus name."

Lucinda fumbled with her Bible. Hadn't she told the Lord last night she didn't want any changes? The pastor spoke on how easy her life will move in a different direction if she held on to God's word and believed.

She noticed that Matt and the other worshipers stood. She rose from the pew. The message made her uncomfortable. If only, there was a way she could avoid difficult situations.

"That was a powerful sermon." She walked beside Matt.

"Yes, it was like your pastor knew I'm battling with unnerving decisions."

"I imagine a lot of people are." She picked up her pace.

They continued down the hallway to the Sunday school classes to get Faith. As Lucinda watched her child, she silently asked God to guide her, the way he had Joshua. She wasn't heading into a bloody battle, but the unknown scared her even more.

CHAPTER SEVEN

Matt stayed close to Lucinda as Faith hobbled toward them with a bag in her hand.

"Mommy, I have a surprise." The child glanced at Matt, than eyed her mother as she held up a package.

"What's this?"

"I made it for you." Faith's eyes shined with her gleeful announcement.

"Let's go to the car where I can open it in private." Lucinda leaned down and hugged her child.

Matt assisted Faith to the vehicle. Then he scooted in the passenger side. He grinned at Lucinda holding the bag. "She was very adamant to come this morning to finish your surprise."

"You knew about this?" She opened the present.

Matt paid attention while Lucinda took out a multicolored frame made of Popsicle sticks. He presumed it to be about the size of a calendar. She gazed at a picture of her and Faith centered inside the square. Over the photo was a handwritten verse "Wherefore comfort yourselves together, and edify one another, even as also ye do. 1 Thessalonians 5:11." More wording was beneath the snapshot with each letter a different color. Lucinda read the child's writing. "We can do anything as long as we have Jesus." Lucinda wiped at a tear.

"Mommy, you okay?" Faith squirmed in the seat.

"Yes, this is the greatest gift I've ever received." She turned and kissed her daughter. "I love it. I'll hang it on the wall as soon as we get home." Her attention went to Matt. "And thank you for helping her."

Lucinda started the car and pulled into the traffic. She glanced in the rear view mirror at her child.

"Matt. Will you stay and eat with us?"

He shook his head about to decline.

"Do join us." Lucinda added.

. . ⧈ . .

THE TABLE WAS SET WITH Faith's favorite staple. Matt seated himself and inhaled the aroma of roasted baby potatoes and corn casserole. Eager to dig into a home cooked meal he watched as Lucinda placed rolls and fruit wedges on the table.

"I'm starved." Faith announced.

Lucinda lightly laughed. "Let's say a blessing first."

Matt took a quick look at them and bowed his head. He waited for Lucinda, but Faith spoke up.

"Mommy, can I say the blessing."

"Yes, please honey."

"Jesus thanks for healing my foot. I specially thank you for Matt. He's a good helper. I think he likes Mommy. Amen." She quickly added, "And thanks for my meatloaf."

He raised his head and looked across the table at Lucinda. Pink highlighted her cheeks from Faith's words.

"You're right. I like your mom. I also think you're a very special little girl." He reached to his side and patted her hand before he accepted a roll from the breadbasket Lucinda offered.

Matt tasted the meal. "Mmm. This is delicious. It tastes just like my mother's dish." He stabbed a potato with his fork and took a look at Faith and Lucinda, "Ladies, thanks for inviting me."

"You're certainly welcome to join us anytime. Isn't he?" Lucinda directed her question to Faith.

"Yep." Faith stabbed at a potato with her fork.

During the rest of the meal, he listened to Faith outline the process of making Lucinda's gift. When everyone was finished eating Lucinda pushed out her chair.

"Faith, why don't you go in the living room with your teddy bear?"

"Okay, Mommy." She stood, then limped a few steps to Matt's chair to put her arms around his neck.

"You were a good helper." She whispered in his ear. "Mommy was surprised."

Matt eyed the child as she maneuvered her crutches to leave and turned toward Lucinda. "May I offer my assistance?"

"No, but thank you, I'll load the dish washer later. I hope Faith doesn't make you uncomfortable." She turned to face him.

"When I came here I didn't understand children. This has been a learning experience. Faith is a sweet little girl.

He circled her in his arms. "We adults often censor our words. Kids don't." He leaned down, cradled her face between his hands and lightly kissed her. Matt heard her moan as he ran his hands down her back, drawing her closer for a deeper embrace. Seconds later, she moved away.

"I see how you can write all those intimate scenes." She pressed her lips tight. Worry lines formed on her forehead. "You're a man of the world."

"I'm not a playboy. It's been a while since I've wanted a relationship with a woman. I can't explain this, or us." He took hold of her hand. "All I know is that I care for you."

"I have more to think about than just me." She sighed. "Faith's happiness is important. She's a part of my life." She walked toward the back door. "You'll be leaving in a few weeks to go home. What then?"

"Can't we take it one day at a time? I know things started on a rough note with your daughter and me. But I'd never do anything to hurt either of you."

Matt watched Lucinda open the door and motion for him to leave. "I should check on Faith. But we do need to talk. Will you come back after I put her down for the night?"

"Of course." He gazed into Lucinda's eyes, with a soft stroke, ran his finger across her lip.

. . ❧ . .

A FEW HOURS LATER, clouds overspread the darkened sky with a fluffy film. Matt strolled in the direction of Lucinda's house and scanned the grounds. Weeks ago, he would have never believed that a walk through a field would be preferred to his normal jog in the park. He revisited the day he'd spent with Lucinda and Faith. *Another change.* That idea brought to mind the pastor's message. Nothing stayed the same, but never did he expect to be torn between his life in Washington and the hometown he'd said goodbye to years ago. Nor, had he expected that a countrywoman and her kid could control his heart.

Matt stepped up on the patio and knocked. Through the blinds, he watched Lucinda approach.

"Hi, again."

"Matt." She opened the door wide. "Come in. I have a fresh pot of coffee. Would you like some?"

"Yes, that would be nice." He waited as she poured cups of coffee and spooned creamer in hers. She offered condiments.

"No." He held up his cup. "I like it this way."

"Let's relax in the living room." She led the way.

Matt seated himself next to Lucinda, and then sat his cup on the coffee table on top of a coaster. He leaned against the back of the sofa and put his arm around her. A smile met him as he played with a lock of her hair. "Lucinda, the sermon we heard hit home for me. I'm facing a lot of changes." He moved closer and reached for her hand. "Some concern me."

"What are they?" She took a quick look at their entwined hands. "Is it your writing?"

"Some, not all." He sipped the brew. "I've been thinking about switching genres, but that's the least of it."

"It's you." He put down his cup and embraced her. "I'm falling in love. Each day the feeling is growing..." He kissed her. "And Faith has wormed her way in here too." He touched his chest and then coaxed her into his arms in a passionate embrace. The kiss grew intense before he felt her slip from his grasp.

"Matt." She took a deep breath. "I've tried not to care for you. I've even told myself that I was only charmed because you were one of my favorite authors. When you carried my daughter to me the other day I realized how I felt." She tucked her hair behind her ear. "It's been a long time since I've cared this way about a man, but there are things you don't know about Faith.

"We have time to share our past." He stared at her lips before embracing her again, and then put his arm around the back of the sofa draping it over her shoulder. "I have to go back to Washington for a few days. I need to talk to my agent in person." He smiled. Like a rock, awareness hit him. He was outlining the beginning of something foreign to him. "I've done things I shouldn't have, some involve women. I stepped away from my morals but I want to become an honorable man in all things, especially relationships."

She stood. "This is rather sudden, don't you think?"

"Not really. I knew the first day I arrived that you were special."

"I need time." She shook her head. "It's overwhelming right now. Please, go. I have to think."

Matt stood and gazed at her. *Not the reaction I expected.* "Okay. You know where to find me."

. . ⚘ . .

LUCINDA LISTENED AS his footsteps faded. His vow of affection caught her off guard. Even though his words still rang in her ears the notion that she didn't tell him what would really change his life nagged at her.

Minutes later, she strolled to her room and kneeled beside the bed. "Heavenly Father, I have to make things right." A verse from 2 Chronicles flooded her thoughts "Be ye strong therefore, and let not your hands be weak: for your work shall be rewarded." She shut her eyes tight and wiped moisture. "Matt will be furious with me."

• • ❧ • •

TWO WEEKS PASSED. MATT typed feverously on the last three pages of a chapter. He'd convinced himself that the promise of a new beginning in his career was the reason for his breakthrough. After all, he couldn't move forward until he finished this commitment. He closed his manuscript and debated his writing.

He opened his mailbox and composed an email to his agent outlining a plan for a new book, in a different genre. While he hit send, Matt mentally went back to the day he'd arrived in Black Mountain. He replayed his last evening with Lucinda. *Something wasn't right.* She *seemed distant. Still, being back in my hometown has given me a new vision.* Matt grinned. Women, they had their moods, but he could get used to it. His phone buzzed. He looked at the screen. If only he could conjure up everything by thinking.

"Hi beautiful."

"You sound like you're in a good mood today." He listened to Lucinda's soft tone.

"I'm on a roll with my story and just emailed my agent with an idea for a new book."

"That's good. I'm sure you have a wonderful conclusion planned for the series."

"It'll work out." He leaned back in his seat and raised the front chair legs up from the floor. "I want to concentrate on us. Let's have a late dinner, after Faith goes to bed."

"No. I can't. I haven't been completely honest with you about some things in my past. There's a situation I need you to understand."

"None of us are angels. You're the one who has been talking to me about Jesus." Matt's chair thumped as he put the legs even with the floor. "You said that if the Lord forgives then we become a new person. Our sins are washed away. So you don't have anything in your past to feel guilty about. Me, on the other hand," He shook his head. "I need to seek God more."

"Yes, that verse is in 2 Corinthians, but even Christians have to make things right if it involves others. I expect you'll be unhappy with me. She paused for a second. "Faith is going to a birthday party Friday night with Cynthia. Until then, we shouldn't discuss our relationship. I'll be busy a few days, but I'll see you on Friday."

Matt laid his cell phone down. "What on earth." He wrinkled his brow. *She's never been married and has a child. The things she did in the past shouldn't make any difference. Friday.* He shrugged. Guess he'd find out what she thought was so important that it would make him not want to be around her.

CHAPTER EIGHT

Matt pushed the swing. It moved in a harmonic squeak while Faith giggled. After four weeks of Faith being in her cast, she was bored. He grinned at the surprised expression on Lucinda's face when he offered to entertain her daughter. He kept an eye on the back and forth movements of the swing and speculated. Did Lucinda's feelings toward him teeter, like Faith's swing? All week long, he'd debated over their last conversation and wondered why Lucinda thought an affair with her old boss would make a difference in their relationship.

A truck with a store logo pulled into Lucinda's driveway. A man hurried to her door. Seconds passed. By their hand gestures, he surmised the guy was picking up a load of pumpkins. With Thanksgiving coming next week and his manuscript completed, he needed to leave for Washington in a few days.

Shortly Matt gave the swing another push. His reflections steered to Lucinda. She acted strange toward him and brought doubt into his mind. *Should I return to Black Mountain?* He eyed Faith. Her long hair swayed in the wind. This vacation was certainly a learning lesson. Since being back home, he made a decision to venture out with his writing, and he'd discovered children weren't as obnoxious as he'd once thought.

Matt mentally counted the time he'd been back. So much had changed since the first day he'd pulled into Lucinda's driveway. He felt like a different man, one with a desire to seek more out of life, than just fame. *Lord, Guide me.* A scripture flowed in his mind. "But seek ye first the kingdom of God, and his righteousness; and all these things shall be added unto you."

Faith's cry grabbed his attention. "Matt stop."

He slowed the movements and helped the child stand. "Are you tired?"

"Thirsty." She held on to Matt's leg for a prop.

"Let's get you inside." Matt gathered her crutches and supported her as she hobbled to the house.

"Lucinda?" Matt opened the door and raised his voice.

"Come in." Lucinda met them.

"This little one is thirsty and tired." Matt lifted Faith up the step.

"A snack and some milk should do the trick." Lucinda led her daughter to the table.

Matt longed to ask Lucinda if she'd given any thought to them moving toward a stronger relationship. He watched her give Faith an apple.

"Cynthia will be over later tonight to drop off her uncle's debits and credits. She's hoping you'll autograph one of your novels."

"I don't mind. What time should I come back?" He stuck his hand in his pocket.

"Around six."

"I'll see you then." He turned to leave, wishing he could put his arms around her.

"Matt." She stopped him at the door. "Remember, I mentioned I have to talk with you?" She lowered her voice. "About us."

"I'll be here." He nodded.

He followed the driveway to the end and headed toward his tiny house. He kicked a small rock from his path and then scanned the cloudless horizon. "Lord, I haven't called on You in a long time. Shoot, I've walked away from Your mercy. For that, I'm sorry. I don't deserve it, but you know my heart. I love her."

• • ❧ • •

FINISHED. Matt looked at the counter on the word document and noted seventy-nine thousand, four hundred and fifty six words. Shorter than his usual novel length, but it fit within the guidelines and the ending worked. The Washington Chronicle series was completed. He saved the file, backed it up on a flash drive and opened his mailbox to send the manuscript off to his agent. They had a tentative date to meet at his favorite coffee house when he got back. No doubt, she'd have a few more editorial suggestions for him. He added, "done" to the subject line and sent his message.

After a brief stretch and a can of cola, he sat down at his laptop and opened another document. "Twenty Eight Seasons" He re-read the synopsis. If his research was correct, that was the amount of times, the book of Ecclesiastes mentioned change. He created a new page and outlined plot ideas that would take his main character from the worst of times, to the best, as he battled...*what?*

Matt stopped typing. He needed to figure out the perfect hardship, to triumph scenario. He laid his arm on the tabletop, tapped the surface and noticed it was time to hike to Lucinda's house and autograph a book. He grabbed his jacket and silently anticipated an evening with a promise toward a future. He stopped putting his arm in the sleeve of his coat as reality hit him. *I want a life with her and Faith.*

.. ⁓ ..

LUCINDA TOOK THE FOLDER from her friend. "I'll work on this later."

"That's fine." Cynthia pulled a paperback from her oversized purse. "I can't believe all these weeks you've had Matt Hew right here in your back yard. You've even entertained him at dinner." Her friend's face lit with happiness.

"Don't forget the ice cream." Lucinda laughed. "He made me nervous at first, but he's really a down to earth man." She offered her friend a seat.

"From the way you've talked, I get a feeling you like him."

Lucinda laid her hands on the table and sighed, "I do. Even though, we've only known each other for a little while. Matt says he cares for me too. I don't know if anything serious will happen. His life in Washington is important. It's his livelihood."

Cynthia's brow creased. "He can write books from anywhere." She turned the back over and eyed Matt's biography.

"You're right." Lucinda took a deep breath. "There's more to it than that." She stared at the pepper on the table. "I need him, to understand something about my past before we can think about a relationship."

"Don't look so sad. Trust the Lord in all things, remember." Cynthia added. "Hey, I know what will lighten your spirits. Let me share my latest goof-up."

Lucinda glanced at her friend as she told about going to her uncle's store in a rush. The story progressed and she tried to hide her smile.

"It's okay." Cynthia grinned. "It's funny now, but at the time I was a little embarrassed. There I stood, one black shoe, paired with navy blue. That will teach me to dress in a hurry."

Lucinda chuckled along with Cynthia, as she ended her tale of misfortune about the mixed-matched pair of ballerina flats. "I'm sorry. I'm sure it wasn't humorous at the time."

Cynthia looked up at the ceiling and shook her head "I've done a lot of odd things." A knock mingled with more laughter.

"That's Matt." Lucinda welcomed him. "Hi."

He stepped inside, "Ladies, hello."

"Matt, I know you've met Cynthia. She's been a Godsend to me."

Cynthia grinned. "Shucks, I haven't done anything, except be a friend."

"I'm glad you're in my life." Lucinda added, and looked at Matt. "She's read your books for a couple years."

"I appreciate readers like you." He grinned with his best fan-pleasing smile.

The three of them chatted about books and the retirement of Matt's parents.

"Mommy." Faith's voice traveled to the room.

"I need to help her get dressed for the birthday party." Lucinda glanced at Matt and Cynthia. "You two talk. I'll be back soon."

"Where do you get the ideas for your books?" Cynthia questioned as Lucinda walked away.

"Inspiration can come from a story on the news, overhearing someone's conversation or from people watching."

"Really? You get ideas from seeing others." She put her finger to her chin.

"Sure. Have you ever noticed how people act as they go about their routine? All it takes is a little imagination, questioning what their motives are." Matt briefly looked past her.

"I've never paid much attention. But, there was a time I noticed someone squatting down looking at a crack in the sidewalk and wondered why."

"Yes." Matt ran his hand through his hair. "Those kinds of things can make your imagination flow."

He answered a few more of the same questions most readers asked. Cynthia probed him about his last book in the series. He mentioned the blurb he planned to use on the back cover.

The click, click of crutches sounded in the room. Matt turned to see Faith carrying a present wrapped in bright green paper and decorated with flamboyant birthday wishes scripted in gold.

"Matt!" She flung her arms around his neck. "Are you coming to the party?"

"I can't. You'll be the prettiest princess there." He patted her back as she tightened her hug.

"Thanks." She moved back. "It's Jared's birthday. He's turning three." The child held her fingers up.

"Great. Have fun and eat lots of cake and ice cream."

Lucinda held out Faith's coat. "Please, don't tell her that. She'll be on a sugar high as it is."

"Matt, will you be here when I get back?" Faith's arm went limp as she let her Mom guide her into her jacket.

"Probably not. I'll see you another time though."

"Promise?" The child eyed him.

"Honey, it's time for you and Cynthia to go." Lucinda looked at her friend.

Cynthia opened the door and assisted the child. "Yes, we need to leave, or we'll be late."

Matt stood and waved when he saw Faith raise her hand in a back and forth motion.

"She's a special little girl."

"I think so." Lucinda crossed her arms.

"Is everything okay?" Matt noted her posture and stepped closer. In a quick movement, he lightly kissed her. When she responded, he let his caress linger until she pulled away.

"Whatever is going on, we can sort it out. You wanted to talk."

"It's important." She took two cups from the cupboard, filled them with coffee and handed one to him.

"Let's go to the living room." She led the way to the sofa.

"I've prayed, ever since I discovered," She shook her head when she realized she wasn't making sense. "I didn't know what to do."

"I don't understand what you're talking about." Matt sat his beverage down. "You found out something that's upsetting?"

"It's going to be hard to make things clear." She sipped her coffee.

"Start at the beginning." He grasped her hand and gently squeezed her fingers.

"The beginning." She turned her mug to her lips and then set it on the table. A bit of the brew splashed.

"Promise me you'll listen until the very end before you make any comments. Once I start explaining I don't want to stop." She pushed her hair from her face. "This is the hardest thing I've ever had to do."

"Okay." He nodded, creases formed between his eyes. "I'll listen, ask Faith, I keep my promises." He grinned in an attempt to lighten the mood.

A blank stare met his. He was reminded of a squirrel that stopped in front of his car one day while traveling.

"Sonya Davies was my friend. She came to New York in hopes to find a cure but it was too late." She exhaled, "Matt, she wanted to live, for herself and for her child. She was pregnant." The muscles in Matt's jaw twitched.

"During the last few weeks of Sonya's life she begged me to take her child and raise her. She didn't want her baby growing up in foster care, the way she had. I asked about the father. She told me he was sure to be famous and that a baby would mess up his future."

"I guess, I figured her and the father had discussed things." She paused and swiped her hand over her face. "Sonya requested a lawyer and signed rights to the baby over to me, similar to that of a surrogate mother." She put her hand in the air to stop him when he opened his mouth to speak.

"Matt, she died an hour after giving birth. I planned to let the authorities find the child's father but when they put Faith in my arms, I fell in love. From then on, all I could think about was her happiness. I took Faith home, placed the sealed birth certificate in a box and planned my best friend's funeral. The years passed."

She glanced into Matt's eyes for a sign of recognition. "The next time it crossed my mind was the day we were talking about her going to kindergarten." She picked up her coffee, her expression fixed on him. "Matt, you're Faith's father."

"What?" He gave her a slack-jawed look. "I don't understand."

"You and Sonya created a life together."

"You should have told me earlier." He stared at Lucinda, his eyes constricted as he stood.

"Didn't you listen?" Her voice squeaked. "I only found out myself, recently."

"No. You discovered weeks ago. How dare you control my life by keeping it from me?" He scowled. "I need time to think."

Matt turned away, and then faced her again. "Be assured," He pointed his finger toward her. "We'll talk about *my child* later."

CHAPTER NINE

The sun peeked over the horizon. Matt tossed the key to the tiny house on the counter and slammed the door. In the car, he drove past Lucinda's, grateful that she and Faith were asleep.

The main section of town came into view. A flashing light announced a pancake house. He steered toward the parking lot to go inside.

"May I help you?" Matt turned to the waitress.

"I'll have coffee and a bagel."

"Okay." The waitress smiled and jotted his order.

The scenery on the wall drew his attention. He concentrated on the large oil painting highlighting the fall season with a hay wagon full of fruit. The multi-colored gourds reminded him of pumpkins. Thoughts from the winter produce spilled to Lucinda.

Matt slightly grinned as his bagel was placed in front of him. "Thanks." He bit into the whole-grain breakfast.

"I was wrong." He mumbled. "Lucinda never had a baby." *Faith is my daughter.* Those words blew in his mind like a hurricane.

He put his bagel aside and stared out the window. *Change.* He would always know this place as the city where adjustments occurred. His relationship with Sonya, his first love marked his leaving and now he faced the news of fatherhood. That defined his return. *Would Faith like Washington?* He swallowed the last of his coffee, wiped his mouth on a napkin and laid a twenty-dollar bill on the table.

Matt pulled onto Main and headed out of town. He needed to talk to his agent and close the loose ends on his book. Then he'd plan the rest of his life with his child.

He passed Mason Street, and remembered the last time he saw Sonya. They had enjoyed a wonderful meal and afterwards relaxed in front of the fire. He was certain that was the night his life changed, only he hadn't realized.

He continued to reminiscence and drove by the church he'd visited with Lucinda and Faith. Matt eyed the man outside. The hood of his car was raised. He turned his head as he passed the big brick building and decided the person looked like the pastor. He slowed, made a U-turn and drove into the parking lot to see if he could assist.

"Is everything all right?" Matt approached.

"The battery is dead. I just bought this thing." The man straightened.

"You're Lucinda's friend." Pastor Lamoure grinned and wiped dirt away from his hands with a rag that lay on his fender.

"Can I call someone for you?" Matt motioned toward the car engine.

"No, I have the parts delivery truck coming with another battery." The church leader shook his hand. "Thanks for stopping. Not a lot of folks still do that."

"I was raised to be polite." Matt's monotone comment filled the space between them.

"Son." Pastor Lamoure shut the hood. "I don't mean to pry. You sound a little bleak. Is everything okay? I'm a good person to talk to, despite what my wife says." He chuckled at his inept attempt to brighten Matt's mood.

"Women, right." Matt grinned at the pastor.

"Yeah, but a man needs a good soul mate. Proverbs says, "whoso findeth a wife findeth a good thing." My wife is the best. Well, enough about me. Care to share?"

"Not much to say." Matt shifted his weight.

"Oftentimes a little is a lot. Let's sit on the bench." The church leader pointed to a wooden seat a few feet from them.

Matt walked behind and rested next to the thin haired man. He let out a breath and watched Pastor Lamoure.

"I grew up in a church." Matt ran his hand through his hair. "I've always had God-fearing parents but..." Seconds passed. "Pastor I've sinned. The consequences affect more than me."

"Hmm, I see." Pastor Lamoure nodded. "That's the lineage of sin. It never hurts only the sinner. It always includes others. The important thing is to make things right with God and with the ones you hurt."

"What if someone is gone and I can't make it right with them?"

"Then you make it right with Jesus. He takes care of the rest." The older man looked toward the parking lot to a panel truck that pulled near his car. He took out a business card. "Call me. Remember, nothing is too bad to be fixed, especially if Christ is on your side."

"Thanks, Pastor." Matt took the card and slipped it in his jacket pocket.

"I need to go. I have a long drive ahead of me."

The pastor moved toward the part's truck. "Give your situation some thought and call me. I promise that when the Lord steps in, situations work out for the best."

• • ❧ • •

AFTERNOON CAME AND Lucinda pressed end on her phone. She didn't expect Matt to take her call so she left a message. She took the brownies out of the oven. The scuffle of crutches made her turn.

"Mommy, are you going to make pumpkin pies for Thanksgiving?"

"Sure, we'll eat at Cynthia's house this year." Lucinda turned off the stove.

"What about Matt? He needs to have Thanksgiving." Faith tugged on her mother's shirt.

"Honey." Lucinda bent down on one knee to be eye level with the child. "Matt went back to Washington."

"No." Faith's voice cracked. "I don't want him to go. He needs to stay here, with us." A tear slipped down her cheek.

"I'm sorry." Lucinda cradled her child. "There's something about Matt that I must tell you." She kissed the top of her head. "Later."

"Tell me."

"I will shortly." The phone buzzed. Lucinda glanced at the screen. "Go in the living room. We'll talk about Matt soon."

"Hi." She answered her cell and watched as Faith made her way out of the kitchen.

"Hey, you rang?" Her friend snickered at her comment.

"I did earlier this morning." Lucinda looked to see where Faith was and added, "I need to talk to a friend. Alone"

"You know I'm always here. Why don't you come over and we can chat while Faith plays with the new puppy we bought."

"Puppy?" Her announcement surprised Lucinda.

"Yeah, I know I said I didn't want the hassle with the baby but when I saw him I couldn't say no. James is set on our child having a pet." She laughed.

"What kind is it?"

"It's the cutest black and white beagle you've ever seen."

"I'll bet." Lucinda laughed at her friend's enthusiasm. "I guess we can come over. What I need to talk to you about is confidential. It's important that it be kept between us. Not only do I need a friend's perspective, but I want advice seasoned with faith."

"Of course. Come over in an hour."

· · ✿ · ·

"MOMMY, I HOPE THE BABY doesn't cry."

"Cynthia has a new puppy. It'll be fun." Lucinda rang the doorbell.

"Come in." Her friend greeted them. "Faith, James has the baby in the play room. He's going to hang out with you guys and show you the puppy. He's full of energy. Can you help tire him out so he'll take a nap?"

"Yeah." Faith grinned and hurried to the back of the house.

"My hubby was nice enough to offer his babysitting service so we can chat confidentially."

"I appreciate this." Lucinda took off her coat and hung it on a peg in the hallway.

"Let's go in the kitchen." Cynthia turned toward an arched wall.

"Sit. I'll get us a glass of tea."

Lucinda moved the chair back and slumped into the padded seat. The idea of spilling her secret weighted her down like an anvil. She reached for the glass and waited for her friend to join her at the table.

"I brought the Bible." Cynthia laid God's Holy Word on the table. "We may want some scripture back-up. What's on your mind?"

"I feel like a heel because I've kept a part of my life from you." Lucinda eyed her friend. "It's something that happened before I came to Black Mountain."

"We all have history. I know we've been close for several years but often our past doesn't always seem necessary to share. Shucks, I have things in my history I don't talk about."

"Yeah, but this is mega, it's turned into a problem that can hurt others." The side of Lucinda's mouth twitched.

"I can see it has you upset." Let's remember God is bigger than any problem we have."

"I know. Without the Lord, I'd be lost. Lucinda sat straighter. "Cynthia, I didn't give birth to my daughter." She sipped her tea and waited a second to let the cold blend calm her. "Faith's birth mother was my friend. She came to NY to see a specialist, but her cancer was terminal. Before she died, she pleaded with me to take Faith and be her mom. It was all done legally in the hospital. I didn't know who Faith's father was. I didn't think to check the birth certificate, until recently." She bit the lower part of her lip. "That was a stupid mistake but at the time I was upset and had a new baby to be responsible for."

"Wow." Cynthia rubbed the side of her face. "You're a brave woman to take on a child without help."

"Well, the plot thickens, as Matt would say." Lucinda shook her head wishing things were different. "Sonya Davies was her mother."

"Davies?" Cynthia wiggled her mouth. "She used to live here?"

"Yes, I stayed with her when she was in the hospital. She was alone. I was all she had. Sonya spoke a lot about this area. By the time she died I was charmed with the little town and figured if Faith's mother liked Black Mountain, it would be a good place. Not too long after the funeral I moved here and bought my little farm."

Lucinda put her head in her hands. "Sonya was Matt's first love. Faith is his child."

"Ooh, no!" Cynthia's eyes grew large.

As the silence saturated the room, Lucinda wasn't surprised by her friend's bug-eyed expression. "I know. It's a mess."

"Lucinda, you have to tell him."

"I did. He's angry that I didn't tell him sooner. He left before morning. I called and left a message. What if he takes Faith away? I love her. I can't lose my child. I don't know what to do."

"Wait for him to contact you." Cynthia looked at her friend.

"I guess." Lucinda wiped a lone tear from her eyelash. "Pray with me now, please."

"Heavenly Father, we come to you in need." Cynthia reached for Lucinda's hand. "You know all the circumstances that brought Lucinda to this place. Lord, she has a mother's love for Faith. I ask you to move in this situation and soften

Matt's heart. Guide him so that Lucinda doesn't lose her daughter. In Jesus name, we pray. Amen."

"Amen," Lucinda affirmed the petition. "I have to tell Faith. I just don't know how."

"It might be for the best if you do. She needs to hear it from you. I know you're a knowledgeable Christian. Look at some passages that point to a promised solution and pray, using them to guide you."

"I will." Lucinda shook her head. "I should go. It's late. She stood. "Keep me in your prayers."

Cynthia placed her arm around her friend. "You know it."

Lucinda gathered her coat, coaxed Faith away from the playful pooch and headed home. Faith radiated excitement as she shared tales of the puppy and his antics. Lucinda glanced in the rear view mirror at her daughter and smiled. On the outside, she pretended that the little dog was the star of the show. Inside, her mind jumped to possibilities of having to say goodbye to her child.

Night fell and Lucinda tucked Faith in bed. "Sleep well my love."

"Mommy, when is Matt coming back?"

"I don't know." She kissed her daughter's forehead. "Maybe soon, try to get some rest." Lucinda left and partly closed the child's bedroom door behind her.

The wind whirled past the window while Lucinda stared out, into the night. *A storm was brewing.* She eyed the thick gray cloud overheard. "Jesus, please guide Matt's heart." She closed the blind. On the way to her room she paused to admire the Popsicle frame Faith made in Sunday school. She took the photo from the wall and touched the snapshot of her and

Faith. "We can do anything as long as we have Jesus." She placed the art back on the hook. "Faith trusts you. Lord, I must too."

Resting in her room, Lucinda turned the page of the Holy Scriptures to the book of Psalms. "Behold, God [is] mine helper: the Lord [is] with them that uphold my soul." She continued to read and soon found herself dozing. She closed the Bible and leaned into her pillow. Sleep came as restless as the downpour that was going on outside.

She flipped over. A bolt of lightning banged in the distance, just like the door in her nightmare, which slammed when Matt took Faith away.

• • ⚘ • •

A WEEK BEFORE HALLOWEEN Lucinda greeted two high school boys who assisted with the annual fall festival she held at her pumpkin farm. "Thanks boys. I appreciate your being faithful and helping again this year."

She directed them as they assembled the stand which centered the area. Hay bales were scattered about for seating.

Lucinda placed some homemade pies on the counter. "That looks good—it's solid." She glanced around. "The umbrella can go over the front of the stand to help shield the caramel apples from the sun." She pointed to the spot. "We'll place pumpkins on the right hand side like last year."

"Okay." A tall lanky teenager replied.

"I'll keep track of your hours, when you haul pumpkins and other purchases for the customers."

"What time do you want us back?" A short stocky teen asked.

"Around five. Make sure you moms' know I will drive you home about eight-thirty."

"We'll tell them." The taller boy announced as they got on their bikes and waved.

"Mommy," Faith sat on a hay bale. "Are we going to sell caramel apples again with the pumpkins?"

"We are, and mini pumpkin cakes. We may even have cider to go with those fried cakes. What do you think about that?"

"Yeah." Faith hung her head.

"Honey what's wrong?" Lucinda touched her daughter's hair.

"This cast." Her bottom lip trembled.

"I understand that's it's difficult on you this year." She hugged her daughter. "Cynthia is going to watch you, while I'm working the festival. She'll let you hang around with me until she has to go home and put Baby James to bed. Honey it's only this time. Next year you'll be my assistant again."

"I wish Matt were here. He could stay with me." Lucinda picked Faith up. "Matt has some important business in Washington. He can't be here right now."

Banners were placed along the road to indicate the fall festival. Most locals knew the area, but some from out of town came, especially for the event.

"It looks like we're ready to open and not any too soon. Here come some cars now."

The Saturday before Halloween was busy. Many average size pumpkins for the kids to carve were purchased, along with Carmel applies and cider.

The nine o'clock hour approached. Lucinda knocked on Cynthia's door.

"Come in." Her friend spoke quietly. "Faith is on the couch asleep."

"Thanks for watching her. She was so upset because she has a cast on this year." Lucinda glanced at Faith.

"I talked her into helping me make brownies. She enjoyed that." Cynthia walked over the sofa and picked up a throw.

"I'll bet." She laughed. "Faith tries hard, but she sure can make a mess in the kitchen."

"It's fine." Cynthia handed Lucinda the afghan. "You can put this over her. That way you want need to wake her. "Don't forget James and I expect you and Faith for Thanksgiving."

"I'll be here earlier to help with any last minute preparations" Lucinda gathered Faith in her arms.

"Let me open the car door. You have your hands full." Cynthia gently kissed Faith on the head and walked ahead of Lucinda.

$$\bullet \ \bullet \ \infty \ \bullet \ \bullet$$

THANKSGIVING DAY ARRIVED. Lucinda tightened the grip she had on the container of Candied Yams she'd brought, as she rang the bell. She listened to quick footsteps approach.

"Come on in." James took the dish. "Cynthia is in the kitchen."

"Can I play with the puppy?" Faith looked up at him with expectations.

"If it's okay with your mom, we'll go to the play room until the women tell us it's time to eat." He grinned at the child and helped her take her coat off.

"I'll go help Cynthia." Lucinda hung her jacket on the coat peg.

"Everything smells wonderful." She lifted her head to take in the scent of Sage Scalloped Potatoes. "Can I lend a hand?"

"Thanks." Cynthia adjusted her chef's apron. "You can take out the turkey and put the rolls in the oven."

"Sure." Lucinda busied herself with the final dinner preparations.

"How are you doing?" Cynthia paused from stirring the gravy.

"Trusting in the Lord, or trying my best. I don't mind telling you that I'm concerned." Lucinda peeped at the bread. "I just don't know what'll happen."

"I've been praying that it will work out for everyone." Her friend turned off the stove.

"Before this, Matt was actually talking about us having a serious relationship."

"He was?" Cynthia began carrying dishes toward the dining room.

"Yes. He cares for me. I've grown quite fond of him." Lucinda followed with some glasses.

"Really!" Cynthia smiled. "I knew you liked him more than you let on."

"More than I realized." She nodded.

"Lucinda." Cynthia stopped placing the dinner condiments on the table and stared at her friend. "Perhaps, God has a plan in all this."

"I don't know." Lucinda looked ahead in thought. "But the Lord is the only one who can straighten up my mess."

"Speaking of messes." James came in with Faith by his side. "The baby is crying. I changed him but that didn't seem to calm him."

"He's hungry." Cynthia took off her apron and scanned Lucinda's face. "I need to feed my little one and put him down for a nap."

"You go on." Lucinda waved her away. "James and I will get everything ready."

"Thanks guys." Cynthia's words followed behind her as she left the room.

Lucinda organized the dining room for Thanksgiving dinner. Her mind drifted to Matt. A few minutes into the preparation, James touched her on the shoulder.

"I asked you where I should put the pie. You're a million miles away."

"I'm sorry. I guess I was."

"Lucinda, I hope I'm not overstepping my boundaries here. I overheard you say something to Cynthia the other evening about God making things right." He grinned. "I don't know your concern, but I can assure you that Jesus is the problem solver. I'll pray."

"Thanks. I know the Lord will be my guide. It's just difficult sometimes."

Cynthia entered the room with Faith. "I'm famished, and I have a little lady here who says she's hungry also."

"Everything's set." Lucinda scooted the chair out for Faith.

They took their places at the table. Lucinda studied the different dishes of holiday favorites. "This is going to be a wonderful meal."

"It is." Cynthia looked at the table. "We like to say what we're grateful for before we ask a blessing over our Thanksgiving bounty." She glanced at her husband. "My heart is full of thanks for the family I have, and my precious baby boy."

"I'm the one who is blessed." James's face creased with lines. "The Lord gave me a beautiful wife and an amazing son." His face beamed, "Lucinda, how about you?"

"I'm glad that God brought Faith to me. I love her with all my heart." She paused. "I'm appreciative that we have Jesus on our side." She glanced toward Faith.

"I want to thank Jesus for Matt coming to stay on our farm. I want him to come back." Faith grinned. "I love you too, Mommy."

Lucinda patted Faith's hand. They bowed their heads as James said a blessing over the meal.

"Faith gets her cast off next week." Lucinda gave the child a napkin.

"I know you're excited." Cynthia added.

"I'll be glad. I can play outside." Faith took a bite of bread.

They spent the next hour savoring the meal, chatting about the approaching Christmas holiday, and the new additions to Cynthia's household.

• • ❧ • •

AT HOME, LUCINDA CROSSED her arms and observed the sky from her window. The cloudless atmosphere highlighted the twinkling stars. Each one seemed to be taking a turn displaying glittering luster. Until Cynthia's comment, she hadn't given much thought to a future with Matt. *"Oh yes, I do care for him, but Matt and I?"* She pressed her lips together. "Delight thyself in the LORD. He shall give thee the desires of thine heart." She stammered part of a Bible verse and watched the stars dance. "Jesus, only you know that I have desired a relationship with a man whom I could love and who would happily accept Faith? Is it possible?" She stepped away from the window. "Heavenly Father, watch over Faith. Amen."

CHAPTER TEN

Matt raised his Cappuccino mug to his lips. He scanned the customers' faces that were moving about in the Coffee House, while the rich cocoa flavor heightened his taste buds. Some people hurried to start their day. Others enjoyed their favorite drink over the morning news.

His phone vibrated with a message from his agent, *running late*. He typed a fast "*K*" in reply. His first week back in Washington was anything except a relief. When he left Black Mountain, he was sure that being back in his penthouse would give him clarity. He mulled over the fact that he was a father. Someone else was in his life that depended on him. That image fueled his desire to set a good example. He wrapped his hand around his cup. A childhood memory came to mind. He and Dad fished in a pond on a summer afternoon. Later, they joined Mom for a picnic. Matt released an easy breath. His parents were always taking him on adventures to instill the joy of nature in him. He wanted the same for his child.

Matt rubbed his neck. His hand stopped on the spot where Faith had hugged him. When he'd arrived in Black Mountain, he could barely tolerate kids. Spending time with Faith modified his views about children, and she'd found a way into his heart. He finally understood how parents felt when they spoke about their kids with delight. *Love.* The word meant much more than any novel could portray.

He turned his attention from the people inside the restaurant and eyed a black bird from the window. It flew down to the sidewalk and pecked at a piece of discarded bagel. The mid-day sunrays illuminated its feathers. Again, he compared the bird's shiny black wings to Lucinda's long locks.

Matt turned away from the bird and sipped another drink. He'd always prided himself on seeing things clearly, but it had taken him a while to realize that he'd lost his heart to Lucinda. It happened long before he learned he was Faith's father. He wiped his chin while mother and child dominated his mind. "Lord, I want my child. Can I separate them?"

His whispered comment drew the attention of a passerby. He turned from her surprised gaze and spotted his agent nearing the table, her heels clicking against the cement floor.

"Sorry I'm late." She pulled out a chair.

"It's fine. I'm enjoying." He held up his beverage. "I ordered you the usual."

"Thanks." She laid a folder beside her. "I guess being back at your old stomping grounds somewhat refueled your imagination." She paused as the waitress placed her espresso down. "However, your manuscript seemed to have a different voice this time." She wrinkled her brow. "Matt, what has happened? Your first eight novels were more cosmopolitan than this one." She shook her head. "I thought the zest was a little off. Certain chapters were a bit tame." She tasted her beverage.

"I realize this book is toned down, not as much gore." He swallowed the last of his brew. "You know I write the way my impressions take me. For some reason, creating hair-raising violence has lost appeal."

"Well." She exhaled. "It's what your fans anticipate. You can't change now."

"Who says I can't?" His mouth puckered as he eyed her. "I think book lovers understand more than you give them credit for. Maybe a more sensitive approach will get new readers interested too."

"I became your agent because you write for the masses that welcome books with news worthy stories. Plots that shock people and make them thankful they're not there. Those are the readers that I represent. For me, anything else is substandard." She sat her cup down hard. "I spoke to the publisher. He'll accept this last manuscript in the Washington series." She frowned. "Still, if you want to continue to have a working contact, you can't switch your writing style. I hope plans for another story will hold the same pattern you're famous for."

Matt listened to his agent's abrasive tone. His memory traveled back to a scripture his mother used to quote from 1st Corinthians. *"But God hath chosen the foolish things of the world to confound the wise, and God hath chosen the weak things of the world to confound the things which are mighty."*

He placed his empty cup to the side. "You know what I discovered while I was away?" He didn't wait for her to answer. "For years, I've written what others expected from me. I based my entire career on creating novels like the one I inscribed in college. That book was for the shock factor. I did it because I knew it would make me a best-selling author."

"You're where you envisioned, so continue to write the books expected of you." She put her strap to her shoulder bag over her arm.

"No." He shook his head. "I'm going to try plotting a book in a different genre. Maybe, set the scene around a Bible verse."

"What!" Her daggered expression met him. "You go away for a few weeks and now you're suddenly getting religion?" She stood and towered over his booth. "I'm not that kind of agent. If that's your plans, perhaps you need to send a query to Jeff Hanno. I hear he represents writers for those types of novels." Her voice laced with sarcasm. "He calls them uplifting." She put her fingers in the air to make quote signs before she turned and hastily headed for the exit. Matt watched her leave, rose from his seat and tossed his cup in the trash.

He made his way three blocks south, toward his penthouse. At his door, he shook his head with wonder at how a simple meeting could turn into a fiasco. Never had he expected his agent to get vile over the fact that he wanted to tone down his plots.

Later in the day, Matt prepared a load of clothes to deliver to the dry cleaners. He checked his pockets and retrieved the card Pastor Lamoure gave him. He turned the card over in his fingers and deliberated about his life. Before now, he hadn't noticed how he'd moved away from his parents' teachings, or the Lord's grace. *Things of the world can certainly turn you around.* He grabbed his phone, a bottle of water and sat in his favorite chair.

Matt punched the numbers to contact the leader of Black Mountain Church. On the third ring, a man answered.

"Hello."

"Pastor Lamoure. This is Matt Blake."

"Good to hear from you. How are things in Washington? I believe that's where you said you live."

"Yes. It's breezy today. I do miss North Carolina's tempered weather."

A chuckle met his ears. "I'm with you. A calmer climate works best for my old bones."

He grinned at the church leaders comment. "Sir, have you time to talk?"

"Let me close my door for privacy. We can chat as long as you need." Matt heard the rustle of steps followed by a thump. "Son, what's on your mind?"

"Going back to my home town has opened a can of worms, as they say." Matt put his feet up on the cocktail table. "I'm contemplating many uncertain changes in my life."

"The future is always a question mark. I guess you know that I'm going to tell you that with Jesus the way is steadier. I don't mean a Christian's path is easy, just that walking with the Lord makes it better."

"I know. Mom says God is with you where ever you go."

"She's a smart lady. Matt has something else gotten you perplexed?"

"A lot of things," He rubbed his forehead. "My writing, for one. I'm known for creating books with violence. I fell into a slump, a big case of writer's block. That's why I rented Lucinda's tiny house. I'd hoped that being in my hometown would spark my creativity."

"And did it?" Pastor Lamoure asked.

"Yes and no." Matt laid his hand down on the edge of the chair.

"I'm sorry? The pastor paused and added. "I don't follow you."

"Let's just say, I've developed a desire to plot stories with fewer graphics."

"Perhaps, it's part of your growing."

"I don't see how that can be classified as growing?" Matt took a sip of water.

"Many people wouldn't. The Lord does. He calls whom He may, and directs a believer's path." Pastor Lamoure continued, "Jesus was meek, but strong. His ways are not the way of the world. Many believers write as a way to highlight God's salvation. I take that you accept as true, that Jesus is the way to a Heavenly home."

"I do. Earlier today, a verse Mom likes came to mind. It's the one about God choosing foolish things of the world to confound the wise."

"Yes, 1 Corinthians 1:27. I'd take that as a confirmation."

"What do you mean?" Matt sipped his water.

"Any time the Lord brings to memory His Holy Word and someone comments on a similar situation, it's an assurance that God is trying to guide you. Maybe, He's nudging you to use your talent for His glory."

"I hadn't thought of that." Matt bent and took off his shoes. "So, you're saying it's my destiny to change genres."

"I'm only noting that if anyone feels drawn toward something that lines up with God's word, perhaps that's the direction they need to go. Psalms 37:23 and 24 tell us that "The steps of a [good] man are ordered by the LORD: and he delighteth in his way." Sounds like God may be pruning you for better things."

"In more ways than one, I guess." Matt glanced at his tan colored socks and wiggled his toes. "I'm returning home. I recently discovered that I have a child. Some sins can't be hidden."

"Son," The Pastor's firm voice met Matt's ears. "We all fall short of God's glory. I know you've heard that many times. Still, it's as true as it gets. Jesus is ready to forgive and give us a new start. It will be as if no sin has been committed, In His eyes at least. This child you mentioned needs to know you. Babies aren't responsible for the transgressions of their parents. All we can do is give them love and guidance. I want you to pray about our discussion. One day, I hope to see you in church again."

"You may." Matt thought about Faith and her Sunday school class.

"Matt, I remember you said you used to attend church. I assume you've been saved?"

"I accepted God into my life when I was younger." He closed his eyes and leaned against the back of the chair. "I don't know what happened."

"Well, repentance is wonderful. Jesus is waiting."

"My dad has told me the same thing many times. Thanks for the talk, Pastor Lamoure."

"Anytime. You have my number."

Matt ended the conversation and clicked on the television. A local news show was telecasting an accident on Ohio Drive. He shook his head and went to toss his bottle in the recycling can.

Nightfall, Matt opened his laptop and located his document. "Twenty-Eight Seasons." He began to type. Hours passed before he noted the page count. The story had progressed further than he'd imagined. He shut off his computer, stretched and realized it was past midnight. *Faith and Lucinda are in bed.* He strolled toward his sleeping quarters with his mind on the two people who had stolen his heart.

He bent down to slip his shoes in the closet and eyed the chair next to the door. Matt turned toward the seat cushion and put his head in his hands. "Lord, I've sinned. I've strayed from your decency, in a bad way. Please, forgive me. Bring me back into Your graces. In Jesus Name, Amen." Calmness flowed through his body.

Matt breathed in and smiled with assurance that God hadn't forgotten him and lifted up one more request. "Jesus, I love them both. Help me to make the right decision."

• • ❧ • •

MORNING BROUGHT A COVER of clouds. Matt stared out of his patio doors at the dreary day. He rebooted his laptop. Seconds later, he zipped off an email to Jeff Hanno. In his query letter, he gave an introduction and told the agent his plans for writing G-rated books. He mentioned that his current manager suggested he make a connection. He outlined his latest work in progress, attached a synopsis and sent the message.

Man, like a cold rain, awareness of what he'd just done washed over him. If he received a positive response, his life would indeed take a turn. He hit compose again. As if he was talking to the computer he added, "May as well start this off right. I need to respect my fans." He typed a memorandum to one of his contacts who always managed his internet promotions.

Matt summarized his final novel in the Washington book series and closed out the announcement with a few paragraphs to update readers about his plans to embark into a new genre. He exited out of the program, reached for his phone and tapped the screen. Lucinda's voice played, "Leave me a message. I'll call you back."

"Lucinda, this is Matt. We need to talk."

Before noon, Matt finished packing. He looked around his pent house. Earlier, he'd spoken to a realtor in Black Mountain about rental property. One way, or another, he figured he'd stay in North Carolina, for a while at least. He had a daughter and planned to be part of her life.

Before Matt packed his laptop, he turned it on. His Internet mail chimed indicating a message. He glanced at the subject lines and opened his mailbox to see a notice from his agent with a tentative release date and book-signing schedule for the last book in his Washington series. He turned off the laptop and placed it on the counter.

Matt picked up his cell and pressed Lucinda's number again. Her voice mail requested the caller to leave a message. He looked at the phone and frowned.

CHAPTER ELEVEN

Lucinda heard Matt's request to call. She immediately punched his number, only to encounter his recording. She took a deep breath, "Matt. I hope we can work this out so Faith can be happy. Call soon." She closed her eyes and pressed end.

Faith's doctor appointment was over. After weeks of wearing her cast, it was finally off. They went to her favorite pizza place for dinner. When they returned home, Lucinda trotted after her daughter, who jogged around the room to make up for all those times she had to hobble on crutches. "Honey, this is the first day without your crutches. Be careful"

"I'm okay mom. I can run again." The little one gave Mom a cheeky grin.

"I'm glad you can play too, but let's settle down with a movie before bedtime." She put Faith's favorite pink fuzzy oversized pillow on the floor and started a DVD.

Lucinda listened to Faith's youthful glee from the other room as she reached for her phone.

"Lucinda," Cynthia's relaxed tone welcomed her call.

"Hi. Has your day been good?"

"Yeah, but between the baby and potty-training the pup, it's been busy."

"Well at least the puppy will be trained before it's time for baby James, to get out of diapers."

"I hope so." Cynthia laughed. "Did it go well at the doctor?"

"Faith's back to her old self. When we got home, she couldn't wait to run to the door. That girl likes to dash around everywhere. I'm thinking she'll be on the track team in school."

"She is energetic." Cynthia agreed. "Have you heard anything from Matt?"

"I missed a call from him."

"And..." Cynthia paused for an answer.

"Nothing to say, He wants us to talk. He sounded in a hurry. I called back but it went straight to voice mail."

"Lucinda, have you talked to Faith?"

"No." She rubbed her head. "I don't know how to begin."

"I'm as lost as you. Still, it's been just you and Faith. You're the only parent she has ever had, until now. I think you need to tell her, before Matt does."

Lucinda swallowed hard. The feat that stood ahead weighed on her. "You're right. I need to do it soon. I don't know what Matt has planned." From the next room, she heard Faith call. "I better go. I'll talk to you tomorrow."

"Okay. I'll keep praying."

"Thanks." Lucinda stuck the phone in her side pocket and went to look in on her daughter.

"Mommy, the movie is acting funny."

"I see." She scrutinized the picture's squiggly lines and ejected the DVD. "I'll clean it later. It's bedtime anyway." She gently led her child to her room and helped her into her gown.

"I love you." Lucinda straightened the comforter.

"I luv you too, Mommy." Faith's small arms wrapped around Lucinda's neck.

"Let's lay your clothes out for tomorrow." Lucinda rose from the side of the bed and went to Faith's closet.

"I want to wear my princess leggings. I couldn't wear them with the cast on."

"Let's see." Lucinda pulled the pants from a hanger and held them up. "These are lined, they'll be fine." She placed them on Faith's chair. "Your green sweat shirt will match."

She put the child's top on the arm of the chair, strolled over to her bed and sat on the side.

"Honey, I need to talk with you. You're becoming a big girl now. There is something you need to know."

"What?" Faith turned over on her side to face her mother.

Lucinda pushed a strand of hair from Faith's face and recalled the infant with a curl on top of her head. "You've never asked about your father."

"I really didn't think about a daddy until Matt came to stay on the farm." Faith hugged her stuffed bear to her chest. "Matt made me think that's what a daddy might be like. But he's gone away." She pressed her lips together with a pout.

"You'll see Matt again." Lucinda silently asked Jesus to guide her words.

"When Mommy?" Faith voice rose from excitement. "Matt coming back soon?"

"He'll come see you. I'm sure." Lucinda laid her hand on Faith's shoulder. "Honey, Matt is your daddy."

Lucinda watched Faith as she spoke the words. Faith's eyes widened. The child puckered her lips even more and turned over. Seconds passed, Lucinda wondered if she'd understood. She put her hand on Faith's shoulder, and turned her face toward her. "Honey, did you hear me?"

"Aha." She sniffed.

"He left. Daddy not like me?" She shook her head.

"Of course he does. Matt had some important things to do in Washington."

"Oh." Faith turned away and faced the wall.

"I thought you'd be glad that Matt is your Daddy." Lucinda rubbed her child's back.

"I'm sleepy." Faith muttered.

"Okay, you rest. You'll see Matt soon." Lucinda stood and walked to the door. "Goodnight honey. We'll talk tomorrow. You've had a busy day."

Lucinda watched Faith as she stepped past the threshold of her room. She left the door open halfway and went to the living room. While she turned off the lights for the night, she shook her head. Faith's reaction certainly wasn't one she expected. The child was usually full of questions, but tonight she was almost speechless.

She picked up her cell phone and made her way to her sleeping quarters. Later, while she was reading the Bible, her phone chimed.

"Hello."

Matt's powerful voice sounded low. "Hi, how's Faith?"

"She had a busy day getting her cast off." Lucinda massaged her forehead. "Faith is in bed, sleeping."

"I figured it was this week. I know she's happy to have that thing off her leg."

"Yes. She ran for the first time in weeks." Lucinda grinned at the memory of Faith rushing toward the house and heard Matt sigh.

"We need to discuss my daughter."

"Matt, please." She frowned. "I love her very much."

"I know." He hesitated. "I love her too, and you know how I feel about you."

"The feeling is mutual but where does that leave us?" Lucinda closed her Bible and placed it on the side table.

"A day at a time. First, I need to talk to Faith. What did you tell her? Did you mention Sonya?"

"No. I don't believe she's ready for that. I did tell her that you're her father. Are you coming back to Black Mountain soon?"

"Yes and I agree with you about Sonya. It's too much information for a five year old to comprehend. Besides, she loves you. Sonya is gone. You're her mother now. How did she take the news that I'm her dad?"

"She didn't understand why you left. I told her you had something to deal with in Washington."

"Thanks. I'll probably be back late tomorrow evening."

"Matt. I'm glad you approve of me being Faith's mother. That's a start, right?" She turned her face toward the door. "I should go. I think I heard Faith."

"Okay."

Lucinda tossed the phone on the bed and listened, positive she'd heard crying. She made hast to Faith's room and peeked inside. Faith was still and lying on her side, toward the wall. She eased out a breath and pondered her daughter's earlier response. Faith was never speechless. Tomorrow would be different. Her questions would be endless.

CHAPTER TWELVE

att stepped off the elevator inside his penthouse. He took one last glance around to make sure all was in place, not knowing when he'd return to Washington. The realtor left him a message confirming a vacant apartment. Lucinda's tiny house was nice as a vacation stop, but not his choice for a full time home. He grunted and recalled his mother's preference for shows about living in small spaces. He could inform her it wasn't for him. *I need to tell her about Faith.* "In a few days." He spoke his thoughts and sat down to send a message to his new agent. It hadn't taken but a few days for Jeff Hanno to agree to represent him in his new adventure and send him a contract. He glanced at the professionally worded email indicating the need to adhere to clean, inspiring fiction. He rubbed his chin. *Yeah, certainly a different genre.* He opened the attachment and read the agreement, adding his electronic signature. "Lord, I'll need your direction in writing from now on." He hit send.

• • ✣ • •

LIGHTS SHINED IN EVERY room. Matt set his phone alarm and was up long before dawn to make the drive to North Carolina in hopes to get there before noon.

He yawned while the stoplight held him. As he turned left toward the interstate, he pictured Faith's cute smile. How had she reacted when Lucinda told him he was her father?

A few hours into the trip, his phone blinked to inform him that the battery was dead. He plugged it in the car charger and pulled into the parking lot of a sandwich shop to order a quick bite.

With many miles and a few stops behind him, Matt moved his neck sideways to stretch. He passed a police car and pulled into Lucinda's drive. His brow wrinkled as he eyed Lucinda. Her head bowed in her hands. He saw that she was upset and quickly turned off the ignition to rush to her side.

Her wild eyes and sobs sent his heart into double-time. "Lucinda, what's wrong?"

"Faith is gone." She whispered.

"What?" Irritation filed the air. "Where is she?"

"I don't know. She inhaled a broken breath. "The police took a picture of her and are combing the neighborhood."

"Why didn't you call me? Like it or not, I'm her father." He snarled as he ran his hand over his chin. The air was chilly, but his face was a sauna.

"I tried to call." Her words flew out as her tone lifted. "Your phone was off."

"I never turn my cell off." He growled, then turned away when he recalled plugging it in the car charger and going into the fast food restaurant. He sighed and mentally counted to ten in an attempt to calm down when he realized he never turned it back on.

"You're right, my cell was off." He moved closer to her. "Tell me what happened."

"When I woke and went into her room, she was gone. She's never done anything like this before. I don't understand. The officer believes she let herself out and wandered off."

"Did she seem okay when you told her I was her father?" His mouthed winkled.

"Yes, she didn't ask much, but she was worn-out from her day. I figured she'd be ready to question me during breakfast."

Matt moved back. "I'm going to search for my child. We'll talk when I find Faith. Without a doubt, my daughter needs better supervision." His glare fixed on her face.

As Matt headed toward the pumpkin patch he huffed at the cringe he'd witnessed on her face.

CHAPTER THIRTEEN

Fast steps carried Matt toward the tiny house. He explored the surrounding area, and made sure Faith wasn't inside or playing on the stoop with her toys. He paced around the adjoining field and breezed past several ripe pumpkins.

Matt stopped and scratched his head. *Where could she be?* He scanned the acreage for any sign of a child, or a toy. With no plan, he walked the perimeter. The police were searching the neighborhood, and the road toward town. *She wouldn't go that way.* A notion surfaced about his daughter and the things he'd learned in the short weeks he'd known her. *One of her favorite things to do is play in the field.* He came upon a stump and dropped hard on the surface. "Ouch." He flinched when the blistery wood met his behind.

Matt touched his back pocket. Quickly he forgot the discomfort his woodsy seat caused as his mind searched for ideas as to Faith's whereabouts. He looked ahead and caught sight of a cloud gliding across the sky. The heavens above were Carolina blue. He grinned at a saying his dad liked to toss out when the sky was a pale blue.

Matt squinted from the sunlight. It was fall, but the mild temperatures had hung around. He eyed the area, relieved that it was light jacket weather. "Thank Goodness." He eyed another fluffy puff of white and clasped his hands together. "Jesus, keep Faith safe. I've asked a lot recently when I petitioned your pardon for my sins, but please, I'm calling on you now for an innocent child. Help us find her and bring her back safely. Amen." He turned away from the horizon and then gazed at the skyline once more. "Holy Father, I know she's treasured in your sight. She's precious in mine too. I didn't really understand my love for her until now."

Matt balled up his fist and shook his head. "Where can she be?"

A picture materialized in his mind. His awareness went back to the day he found her in the overgrowth beyond the pumpkin patch. *Her hiding spot.* His feet didn't seem to carry him fast enough as he sprinted toward the vine cover cavity that could hide a child.

The creeping foliage wrapped the limbs of the trees. Matt surveyed the twisting maze of ivy, tangled with various other thickets in front of him. The vegetation formed an arch close to the ground, which offered a forestry doorway begging for exploration.

A whine echoed through the trees and drew Matt's attention. He ambled toward the opening and listened. After a short pause, he picked up his steps and squatted to peek in the gap the unruly shrubbery offered. He looked inside and spotted Faith huddled in the corner.

"Princess, are you okay?" Matt crawled inside and leaned on his knees a few feet from the child. "We were worried about you."

"Not you." Faith rubbed her nose and lowered her head.

"Faith, why would you think that?" He tried to scoot closer.

"You left." She looked briefly at him. Faith turned away and mumbled. "You don't like being my daddy."

"Princess, that's not true. I'm very happy to be your daddy. I want us to be together."

"You left. Last night I heard Mommy ask you to come back." Faith bit down on her lip.

"Honey, you may have misunderstood. Mommy wanted to know when I was coming back. I had business in Washington. Having you for a daughter is wonderful."

"Really?" Faith stared at him. Her mouth twisted with indecision.

"Certainly. I want to be in your life forever." He reached out. "Come with me. Mommy is worried about you." After a few seconds, Faith's fingertips touched his. He gently grasped her hand. "Let's get you home. I'll bet you're hungry."

"I might be." Shaky, slow words flowed to him.

Matt moved backward as his child crawled toward him. Once outside he smiled, hugged her and stood. "I'm too tall to fit into that hideaway." He extended his arms over his head.

"Your knees are dirty." Faith giggled as she watched him stretch.

"Ready to find Mommy?" He softly touched her shoulder and guided her toward the house. They passed the pumpkin patch and the field. As they approached the tiny house Matt steered her to the steps. "Sit with me for a minute."

"Why?" Faith studied his face.

"I want to say something." He rested on the highest stair. "Honey, when I found out you were my daughter, I was nervous."

"Why? It's okay, ain't it?" She twisted back and forth.

"I'm very glad about it. But I've never been a daddy and I want to be the best one I can be."

"I think you'll be a good daddy." Faith put her hands on her hips. "If you stay here."

Matt laughed. "I have an apartment in town."

"You can stay here." She pointed to the tiny house.

"It's too small to live in forever." Matt stood. "We'd better go. Mommy is concerned." They walked with a faster pace. Lucinda's house came in view.

When Matt got closer, she turned and saw Faith. Matt stopped as Lucinda ran and cradled Faith in her arms.

"Faith where were you? I was scared." Lucinda grinned at Matt and mouthed "Thank you."

"I was in my playhouse." The child pulled a twig from her sleeve. "I'm hungry."

"We'll get you something to eat."

"Come inside." Lucinda's brows knitted together as she addressed Matt.

"I will." He followed them to the kitchen.

Matt took a seat at the table and watched Lucinda prepare a sandwich. She placed the meal in front of Faith with a glass of milk. As the child dug into the food, Lucinda hugged her. "Lord, thank you for guiding Matt." She glanced sideways.

Matt nodded. "One thing we will do is build Faith a playhouse in the back yard close to home." He touched his daughter's shoulder. "I don't want you going into the woods by yourself ever again." his voice firm. "Understood?"

"Okay." Faith nodded and looked back and forth at the adults.

Matt concentrated on Lucinda and Faith. Minutes passed. She busied herself with catering to her child's appetite. Lucinda sat down. He spoke. "I rented an apartment in town right off Main Street."

"I hope you know that the tiny house is always available." She pushed Faith's empty pudding dish aside.

"I appreciate the offer but living in small space isn't my style for long term housekeeping. Besides, I need an additional room." He looked at Faith.

"Matt. Please. I know things have been rocky but you need to understand."

"I think you need to get this little lady in the bathtub." He stood and kissed Faith on top of the head. "We will talk shortly."

"Honey, I'll be back in a few days." He directed his attention to the child.

"Promise?" Faith raised her voice.

"I promise. Mommy has my phone number if you want to talk to me." Matt passed by Lucinda, in a low voice added. "After Faith goes to bed. We need to discuss a few things."

. . ❧ . .

LUCINDA EYED THE DOOR as Matt closed it. She turned to Faith and grinned, not willing that her child would notice concern on her face.

"Come on. Let's get you in the tub."

Lucinda called the police station to report that Faith was home and apologize for not calling sooner. She gathered her daughter's pajamas and went back to get her ready for bed. Later, she pulled the covers over Faith. "Honey, promise me that you'll never go outside without telling me, especially after dark." She gave Faith a serious look.

"I won't do it again Mommy."

"What made you leave in the middle of the night?" Lucinda frowned.

"I thought Daddy didn't like me." Faith's mouth turned down.

"Honey, Matt thinks you're a great daughter. He just has some things to work out."

"I know. He told me." Faith yawned.

"You get some sleep and stay in bed." She turned off the light.

Back in the kitchen, Lucinda placed the plates and bowls in the dishwasher. She prepared a pot of coffee and noticed the time. *Matt will be here soon.* She glanced outside and spoke in a barely audible tone. "Lord, I don't want to lose my child." She turned away as the sound of a car engine drew near.

Lucinda opened the door before he had a chance to knock. She moved aside to let him in.

"I have coffee, if you'd like some."

"Thanks. I could use a cup. This has been some day." He seated himself.

"It was scary." She offered Matt a cup of java. "I love Faith with all my heart. I hope you realize that."

"I do. He sipped from his mug. "She's your daughter. I understand the Lord entrusted her to you." He took another drink. "She's also my biological child. I haven't known her long, still I love her too." His gaze penetrated hers from over the top of the mug.

"Yes, you're her father. I hope we can work together for Faith's best interest." Lucinda pushed her hair aside. "I haven't heard you speak about the Lord before."

"A lot has happened since I returned to Washington." Matt scooted his chair back and made room to extend his legs. "I spoke with the pastor and later I reconnected with Jesus. I'm even going to try writing something other than secular novels."

"I think that's wonderful and I can't wait to read your new endeavors." She grinned and silently thanked the Lord for guiding Matt to His grace.

Matt gazed at her and recalled the last time they kissed. As much as he wanted to reach out and feel the softness of her lips, he had to think about other things. He pushed ideas about holding Lucinda in his arms away. Decisions had to be made. "Lucinda, I want Faith."

CHAPTER FOURTEEN

Matt crossed his arms at Lucinda's gasped.

"Please, no!" Her hand went to her mouth and muffled her words. "I don't want to lose her."

"I'm not suggesting that I'm taking her from you for good, but I need to spend time with my daughter. Maybe, take her to visit her grandparents." He stood. "You've had her five years. I just found her."

"I don't know." She rose from her seat and paced the floor.

"Lucinda, I'm not asking. I'm telling. I can give Faith as much supervision as you've given her lately."

He noticed her bite her lower lip and shook his head. "I didn't mean to be cruel. I was upset, and scared. I'm just now becoming part of my child's life. My furniture will be delivered tomorrow. I've leased a duplex at Pebble Creek, on the edge of town." Matt walked to the door and opened it. "In a day or so, I should be settled. I'll come get Faith. We need time to get to know each other."

"Matt, stop." She coaxed him to wait. "I agree that you two should get better acquainted but can you tell me how long you plan on keeping her."

"Maybe, for a couple weeks. We'll get a legal contract prepared to share custody. You're welcome to come over anytime." He reached out, circled Lucinda in his arms. Their eyes locked. "You know I care for you. And Faith loves you, beside Christmas will be here in about a month. I wouldn't mess up her holiday." Seconds later, he turned away. Matt longed to kiss her, but he needed to think of Faith first. They were a family.

What should have been a quiet, short drive to his apartment was troubled by the day's events. No sooner had he gotten to his new place and unloaded his luggage he was faced with a missing child. Matt tightened the grip on his steering wheel. *I asked Jesus to forgive me.* He'd nodded, knowing that the acceptance of Christ washed over him. *Now, I'm confronted with all this. What about Lucinda?*

He parked and decided to take care of one hurdle. He walked briskly inside his new home, tapped his phone and waited for Mom to answer.

"Hello, son."

"Mom, hi. Have you and Dad had a good day?"

While he listened to his mom bring him up to date on Dad's new hobby he debated various ways to tell them that they were grandparents.

Matt requested Mom put her phone on speaker and have Dad close. For both of them he recounted the changes in his life, starting with him asking the Lord's forgiveness for straying. Next he summarized Sonya's pregnancy and her request that Lucinda raise Faith. He breathed with relief from his parents delight in knowing they had a five-year-old granddaughter.

"Son, how is all this affecting Lucinda?"

"What do you mean?" He scratched his head at his mom's question.

"She's the only mother the child has known. I know that she loves Faith. I'm sure Lucinda is concerned that you'll take her away for good."

"Oh! I hadn't considered that."

"No son, I doubt you would, but women stay on the same wave length and as a mom I can say…"

He unbuttoned his sleeve while Mom aired her apprehensions about Lucinda's side of the equation. After an hour, he laid his phone down. His mom had requested that he be thoughtful in any decisions that included the child and Lucinda. He thought about the verse Mom had quoted from Ephesians. 'And be ye kind one to another, tenderhearted, forgiving one another, even as God for Christ's sake hath forgiven you.' He went off to shower with his mother's comments pushing for acceptance.

• • ❧ • •

LUCINDA FINISHED A report and shut down her laptop. Faith stood beside her and waited patiently. "Okay, Mom's done. Let's have a snack with a glass of milk. We need to talk." She got an apple pie from the refrigerator, cut two slices and poured glasses of milk. Lucinda took a seat beside Faith. "Let's be thankful. Heavenly Father, Bless our food and watch over us. Amen." She glanced at Faith while she chewed. "Honey, how do you feel about going to stay with Matt for a few weeks?"

"I don't know." Faith forked up some crust. "Will you come too?"

"No." She plastered her best grin on for her daughter's sake. "Daddy wants you two to spend some time together." She pushed her plate away, any appetite she had was gone. "He doesn't live far. I will come over as much as I can."

"I like living with you, Mommy." Faith's bottom lip trembled.

"And that will never change. I'm your mother. You'll only spend time at Daddy's. This will always be your home."

"And you will come over and see me?" Faith went back to eating her pie.

"You couldn't keep me away." Lucinda nodded.

Before night fall Lucinda's phone chimed. She glimpsed the number.

"Hello, Matt."

"Hi, how's the princess doing today?"

"She's back to her old self. Right now she's working on a coloring project."

"And you?" His tone softened.

"I'm fine. Did you get your household belongings?"

"They arrived this morning. I've been arranging furniture and placing contents I had boxed. The first thing I opened was the coffee brewer." He chuckled

"I enjoy my morning java too." She peeked in the next room and found Faith still engrossed with her artwork.

"Yesterday my priority was Faith, but I want you to know that my feelings for you haven't changed. I want us to see where the future takes us."

"Matt, I can't talk about this right now. My mind's going in so many directions."

"I understand. Just pray, okay."

"I will" She scarcely paid attention to his next words as her mind was on prayers that Faith would never leave.

"Lucinda, did you hear me." His voice broke her thoughts.

"I'm sorry what did you say?"

"I'll be there around noon Friday to pick up Faith."

"Oh."

"You know you're welcome to come by."

Thanks, Matt. I'll probably do that because this will be the first time that Faith and I have been apart."

"I don't want to make things difficult. I called Mom and Dad and told them about Faith. I also asked them not to say anything about Sonya. In time, we'll tell her. For now, she needs our love and nothing more."

"I'm glad you agree. Originally, I'd planned to tell her when she became a teen. I have a photo of Sonya and a letter that she wrote Faith a few days before she died."

"It's settled then."

"Yeah, one thing worked out." Lucinda mumbled.

"It's all going to be fine. You'll see. We both want the best for our little girl."

"I'm sorry." As if this was the first time she'd listened to Matt Lucinda noted sincerity in his tone. A peace washed over her. Her anxieties calmed like a waved displacing back toward the sea.

"Matt. I've been thinking about all this, only measuring my needs. You're right we both want the best for Faith. I need to trust you."

"You can be assured that I will never come between you and your daughter."

They chatted for thirty minutes. Matt added. "Will you think about us going out sometime just me and you?"

"I suppose." She smiled still enjoying the new awareness of harmony that engulfed her.

"Good. I'll say good night. May I speak to Faith?"

"Night Matt. I'll give the phone to her.

Lucinda strolled to the other room. "Faith, Daddy wants to talk to you."

"Daddy, where are you?"

Lucinda paid attention to the one-sided conversation. When she heard Faith say goodbye she stepped closer and took back the cell.

"Mommy, Daddy says he will pick me up in a couple days and that you'll come over too."

"Yes, honey. I'll try and stop by every day and Daddy has my number so you can call me."

. . ✿ . .

FRIDAY ARRIVED. MATT took a last minute scan of Faith's bedroom. The canopy bed he purchased was dressed with her favorite princess themed bed linen. In the corner of the room sat a playhouse for her doll, complete with a garage to park the pink convertible that she always pushed around. He made a mental tally of his food supplies. He'd tried to remember the importance of nutritious meals but he had slipped in a bag of chips, a box of popcorn and some cookies. He headed out the door for the three-mile drive to pick up his daughter.

Rain spotted his windshield with sprinkles hard enough for him to turn on his wipers. He pulled into Lucinda's drive, hurried to the door and knocked.

"Good afternoon." He smiled as Lucinda opened the door.

"Come in." She sat her water bottle on the counter. "Faith is almost ready."

He grasped her hand. "After church Sunday come by the apartment the three of us will have dinner." As he extended his invitation, he heard Faith's footsteps. "We'll make Mommy a delicious meal." He grinned at his daughter. "Won't we?"

"Mommy says I'm a great helper." Faith pulled her tote behind her.

"I'll need lots of assistance." He smiled at the child, and motioned at her luggage. "Is that all you're taking?

"No. I have another bag."

"She insisted on taking her Barbie dolls and car." Lucinda bent down and hugged her child. Then went to get the other suitcase

"I'm glad because your dolls have a new house." Matt added.

"They do?" Her voice rose with excitement.

"Sure do."

"Matt, here's her dress." Lucinda held out the outfit. "She'll need something to wear to Sunday school." He took the outfit and looked from Lucinda to Faith.

"Princess, say goodbye to your gerbil while I talk to Mommy a minute."

"Okay." She jogged to the next room.

"Lucinda. I hadn't even considered what the town will think once they find out I'm Faith's father."

"I did." She waved her hand in the air. "I'm used to folks thinking strange things about me. The town believes that I'm an unwed mother, saved by grace. I guess now they think that we..." her words stopped.

"Probably." Lines creased in Matt's face. "Faith is what's important. Perhaps, we should let them assume what they want."

"I'm okay. But you don't know how some folks can be. Even Christians will speak things that they shouldn't sometimes. We may get asked about our past."

"I say we tell them its history, we're beginning a new chapter." Matt gently touched her cheek. "After all, we're both commencing on a road we haven't walked before."

"You're right we are." She took a shaky breath and felt his lips brush hers.

"Mommy." Faith came to a quick halt when she saw Matt and Lucinda hugging. "I got my bear." She grinned and held up her stuff animal.

"Yes, you'll need it tonight." Lucinda backed away and felt her face grow warm.

"Princess, let's go. Mommy can get some work done and she'll see us in church."

· · ❧ · ·

MATT UNLOCKED THE DOOR and carried his daughter's belongings inside. Faith stood over the threshold with her knuckle in her mouth.

"Princess, what's wrong. Come in." Matt touched her back and lightly directed her inside. "Are you okay?"

The child nodded. "I've never been away from Mommy." Her voice quivered.

"Honey." Matt knelt down and hugged Faith. "I promise you that I'm not keeping you from Mommy. I only want us to get to know each other. I love you."

"I luv you, even when you yell." Faith eyed him.

"I'll try not to shout." Matt grinned and stood. "Let me show you what your room looks like. While I'm making soup and sandwiches, you can talk to Mommy."

"Okay." She grinned and followed Matt down the hallway.

"This is my room in case you need me." He pointed to the end of the hallway. He opened the door next to the living room. "A bedroom for a princess."

"Ooh." Faith studied the space. "I've always wanted a bed with a top on it. I saw one in the store for my Barbie." She walked over and touched her bed. "This is a pretty room."

"It's made for you" Matt placed her luggage down and began to hang her clothes in the closet. He glanced at his daughter as she examined the rest of the sleeping quarters.

"What's this?" Faith ran over to the doll house. "I need Barbie and her stuff." She leaped on the bed and dug her toys out of her tote.

"Since you have two houses I thought your doll needed a place." Matt laughed.

"Thanks, Daddy." She gave him a fast hug and ran back to the make believe mansion.

Matt finished hanging her belongings and went into the kitchen to prepare chicken noodle soup and ham sandwiches. He kept his ear tuned to the sound coming from Faith's room. By the vroom noise he pictured her parking her doll's pink convertible in the make believe garage. He served the soup, sat a sandwich next to Faith's plate, and then headed to her room.

"Are you ready to eat?"

"Okay." Faith placed her doll on the teeny-tiny sofa and accepted Matt's hand as they made the way to the table.

Matt scooted the chair out and helped Faith. "I hope you like chicken noodle."

"It's my favorite." She nodded.

"Mine too." He took a seat across from her. "Shall we bless the meal?" Matt smiled at Faith. "Lord, bless this food." He opened one eye and glanced at his child. "Thank you for my daughter, and for her sharing my home with me when she can. Bless her Mommy. Amen." He grinned as Faith small voice added. "Jesus, bless Daddy."

They ate in silence. Faith slurped the last spoonful and laid half her sandwich down. "I'm full."

"That's fine." I'll put the bowls in the dish washer. Would you like to talk to Mommy before bedtime?" He glanced her way as she nodded and pressed Lucinda's number.

"Hi, I have a princess here, and she wants to talk to you." He handed Faith his cell. He tidied the kitchen and overheard part of Faith's conversation about her doll house before she left the table and walked down the hallway. Fifteen minutes later, she approached Matt. "Mommy wants to talk to you." She returned his phone and hustled toward her room.

"Yeah." He grinned.

"A canopy bed! And a doll house with a garage. You're spoiling our child." Lucinda's voice carried a soft tone.

"Not too much. Just long overdue Daddy stuff."

"I understand." She laughed.

"Are you alright? I mean without her there." He lowered his voice.

"It's strange, but I'll be okay as long as I can talk to her."

"Anytime, you know that." He turned off the kitchen light and strolled into the living room. "Sunday will be a challenge for us."

"It will. I'll call Cynthia and have her say a prayer for us. I told her about Sonya."

"Can you trust her to keep it quiet?" Matt tiptoed down the hall, checked in on Faith and went back to his comfortable chair.

"She's good for her word. I needed to confide in someone."

"And I suppose we can use an ally on our side who understands." He grabbed the TV remote.

"You're right."

After a long conversation he ended the call and went to see if Faith was asleep.

· · ❦ · ·

A MOAN WOKE MATT. HE turned on his back and listened. Another whine, he jumped out of bed and pulled on his tee he'd worn to bed with his jogging pants. As he hurried to Faith's room the whimpers became louder.

"Faith, are you alright?" He went to the side of her bed.

"Mommy!" She grabbed Matt around his neck. Her voice trembled as she choked out the words. "I want Mommy."

Matt's shirt became soaked from Faith tears. He inhaled a deep breath and silently petitioned the Lord for help. *What do I do?"*

CHAPTER FIFTEEN

Matt kissed Faith on the head. "Princess, we'll see Mommy at church Sunday." He glanced at her clock hanging on the wall. A crown sparkled on the purple background as the short wand pointed to three. "It's too late to wake Mommy. Can you try to go back to sleep? First thing in the morning, we'll call her. I'll sit in your room for a while."

"Promise?" Faith pressed her lips tight and gave him a doubtful look.

"I'll be right over there." He pointed to the fuzzy, purple dome chair.

"Okay." She laid back and squeezed her bear to her chest.

"Good night." Matt sat in the rounded seat and extended his legs. Hoping, the chair actually held two hundred pounds as advertised. If so, he had twenty pounds to spare. Maybe he'd survive the rest of the morning.

Early morning, Matt's body jerked from a sound. The noise seemed to leap in his lap. He opened his eyes and tumbled on to the floor. Faith stood over him, her little cheeks inflated from surprise. She watched his awkward movements. First, he had to get out of the fuzzy trap that held him captive, and then stand up, provided the cramp that attacked his calf would go away.

"Daddy, you okay?" Faith moved back to give him room to squirm.

"I'm good." Matt's teeth clenched as he wiggled his leg. Like a mad dog the cramp held on.

"What was that noise?" He bit down on his lip to keep from yelling at his muscle spasm.

"I hopped out of bed. It's bouncy." Her white teeth shined from the pleasure of recounting her adventure of her wiggly bed.

"Maybe we won't bounce on the bed anymore? Okay." Matt words were choppy as he tried to understand why his daughter figured she should jump on the mattress.

"Daddy, you okay? You're walking funny." She giggled.

"In a minute I'll be." He rubbed his knee. "Or, after I take a quick shower." He hobbled to the side table, grabbed his phone and pressed Lucinda's number. "Here, talk to Mommy. Let me get dressed. Then, we'll get you ready for the day."

Matt heard Faith giggling as he returned to the living room. He smiled at the happy sound.

"Mommy, here's Daddy. I'll see you tomorrow." She gave Matt the phone.

"Good morning."

"Is it? Faith said you collapsed her chair and walked funny." She laughed.

"I fell asleep in that small round seat of hers. She surprised me. I sort of broke it trying to get out of the blasted thing. It was a purple fuzzy octopus holding me down. Then I took a cramp in my leg." He moved the phone from his ear as Lucinda's laughter increased.

"I'm glad I can make you happy." He chuckled.

"I'm sorry, but it sounds hilarious." She choked down the last laugh and cleared her throat. "Why were you sleeping in her chair?"

"This dad thing is taking a bit of time." He rubbed his chin whiskers and was reminded to shave. "She woke around three this morning crying for you. I told her I'd stay in her room until she fell back asleep. I guess I dozed off too."

"Faith told me she missed me. I assured her I'd see her tomorrow. I am sorry you've had such an ordeal." She giggled. "Little girls' things can be dangerous."

"Ha-ha." He attempted aggravation but couldn't muster up the sound. He enjoyed the banter between them. "I'll have to buy her another chair, one that is big enough to hold an adult."

"You made it past the first night. She'll probably feel more secure tonight."

"I realize it's new to her." He lowered his voice. "Lucinda, I'm looking forward to seeing you tomorrow. Have you given any thought to us going out? Just the two of us, alone? We've spent time together, but it seems we always have a chaperon."

"I'll see if Cynthia can watch Faith one evening." She paused. "But for now, I need you to outline for me what you have in mind. You mentioned a lawyer."

Matt caught a hint of agitation in her tone. "I want to always be part of Faith's life. I'm only thinking about putting a plan on paper. We never know what the future holds. Both of us need to be secure." He let out a breath, "For Faith's protection I'm going to update my will."

"You have a will?" Lucinda's response sped through the airwaves.

"Yes and a stock portfolio." He mindlessly moved a magazine from one side of the table to the other. "As you understand me more, you'll find out I'm a planner, sometimes to a fault. My novels are all bestsellers except for the last. With that comes a responsibility to be prepared, in case something happens. Right now, everything I have goes to Mom and Dad, but with a daughter, I need to rethink my options."

"Oh, I see. I guess I haven't given much thought to what happens if I'm not around."

"It's not a comfortable subject, but when kids are involved it's necessary." Matt rubbed his eyes.

"You're right. Perhaps, I'll get you to steer me in the right direction."

"No problem, text your email. I'll have my lawyer send you an introduction and go over a few things." Matt looked at the doorway and saw Faith. "I think Faith is ready for breakfast and then we'll shop for a chair."

"Did you get a booster seat?"

"I did. No worries, Lucinda I have it covered."

• • ❧ • •

HE AND FAITH ENJOYED a mid-day matinee. The movie was one of Faith's favorites based on an animal that searched the jungle for his sister. After a happy ending they left the theater and went to a local furniture store. He convinced his daughter to get an adult's accent chair to replace the one he'd broken.

That evening Matt held the door wide for the delivery truck with one hand and balanced a take-out pizza box with the other. When the men left he placed the chair in the same spot where the light-weight saucer chair had sat.

"You're room looks complete again. Shall we tackle that cheese pizza?"

"Yeah!" Faith jogged down the hall.

Matt scooted the chair out and helped Faith to get settled. He focused on getting the simple dinner on the table.

"I'm hungry." He placed his daughter's dish in front of her and took a seat. "Let's ask a blessing." He lowered his head. "Lord, bless this meal. Amen."

Faith added, "Amen." Then she watched Matt pick up his slice. "Mommy usually gets half of our pizza with yucky stuff on her part." Faith wrinkled her nose at the idea.

"Really?" Matt raised an eyebrow and grinned at the expression on the child's face. "What kind of stuff?"

Faith bit into her slice and chased cheese with her mouth. After she swallowed, she shook her head. "Grown-up things like mussrooms and olivers."

Matt laughed. "You mean mushrooms and olives?"

"I guess." She continued to eat heartily.

The dishwasher hummed as Matt turned out the light and followed the vroom noise. He found Faith in her room pushing her car into her make-believe garage. He leaned against the door frame and watched the child play, amazed at the imagination of his little girl. Once again, he silently asked the Lord to forgive his youthful indiscretion and thanked God for placing Lucinda in Sonya's life so that Faith could have a good mother. For a brief few minutes, he daydreamed about the raven-haired pumpkin grower and accountant that had captured his attention before he knew about his child. He straightened. "That's it!"

Faith turned at looked at Matt. "What Daddy?"

"Huh." He realized he'd spoken a thought aloud. "Nothing princess, I was only remembering something. Why don't you get out your pajamas? I'll get your bath ready."

He adjusted the temperature of the water and reached for a plastic bottle with a mermaid on it. He poured a cap full of bubble gum scented foam bath in the tub.

"Daddy. I got'em." She held up her nightclothes.

"I've got it ready for you." Matt turned and step across the threshold. "Call me if you need anything."

"I'm okay. I'm a big girl."

"Yes, you are." He smiled and closed the door. As he left her room, he listened to make sure she didn't fall.

In the living room, he flipped the remote listening for any sounds that might signal Faith needed help. He ran his hand over his face. *I care deeply for Lucinda.* "Lord, I don't want to make a mistake, especially now that Faith's involved."

His cell phone chimed a tune that indicated his mother was calling.

"Mom, Hi."

"Son is everything going well with life? Black Mountain is a big change from the fast pace in Washington"

"Yes different, for sure. Many changes are coming. I signed a contract with a new agent. I'm going to try my hand at clean fiction."

"That's wonderful." She let out a breath, something she always did before she smiled. "How's my granddaughter and when do I get to meet her?"

"Faith's fine, she's spending some time with me. I'm debating about bringing her next week."

"Oh son!" His mother's voice perked up. "Call me the day before you come so I can have a gift for her."

"You don't need to get her anything." Matt heard Faith's bare feet thump against the hardwood floor as she sprinted to the living room. He looked up to see her dressed in her PJ's

"I'm done Daddy." Once Faith saw Matt on the phone she pressed her lips tight.

"Mom, can you hold on a minute?" He laid the cell phone down and motioned for Faith to come closer. "Princess, remember I told you that you have a grandmother and grandfather." He watched her nod. "Would you like to say hi to your grandmother?" He grinned when she agreed.

Matt grabbed the phone. "Mom, Faith will say hello to you." He handed Faith the phone. Seconds passed while he paid attention to the one sided conversation. Faith asked where they lived and then told her about her gerbil and her new room at her Daddy's house. She finished talking and held the cell up.

"Mom, I'll call you later."

"Faith sounds like a wonderful little girl. Will you send me a picture of her?"

"In a few minutes. Good night."

He ended the call. "Grandma would like to see you. Can I take your picture and send it to her?"

"Uh-huh." Faith stood taller and smiled so he could capture her image with his phone. As he sent a fast text with the photo attached, she added. "Can I see Grandma and grandpa?"

"You sure can, wait right here." He left the room and came back with his laptop. He patted the cushion next to him. "Sit beside me. I'll show you some family photos."

An hour passed. Matt clicked on different slides while his daughter leaned against him and asked about the snapshots.

"Grandma is pretty." Her small finger touched the screen as she pointed to a picture of Matt's mother.

"Yes, she is a nice looking lady." He took a gander at the representation of his mother as if seeing her for the first time. Her hair was styled with curls. The smile she wore showed perfect white teeth. She stood beside him in one of her best outfits. "This was taken when Grandma and I were at her brother's wedding."

"Wedding?" Faith eyes widened. "I thought young people married."

Matt laughed. "They do. Older folks sometimes get married again too, if something happens to their spouse."

"Why?"

He chuckled and shut the lid to his computer. "People fall in love. Age doesn't matter, once you're grown." He grinned at Faith. "Are you up for helping prepare a meal for Mommy tomorrow?"

She hopped off the sofa and nodded. "Mommy likes spehetti"

"Pasta? I had something else in mind." He stood in the kitchen and eyed the steak he'd purchased.

"I like spehetti too. Please."

Matt grinned at Faith. Her eyes begged. "How about baked spaghetti? We can warm it in the oven tomorrow."

She glanced around the kitchen, "If it tastes like Mommy's."

"You'll like it. Can you get the cheese?" He laughed, and began to gather the rest of the ingredients.

Matt cracked the eggs with his daughter taking in every step of the process. Thirty minutes passed. Finally, he and his little chef had a casserole prepared. Matt placed the meal in the oven.

"All we have to do now is let it cook. I'll toss a salad tomorrow." Matt turned the timer on. "What about dessert?"

"Do you have ice cream?" Faith stretched her head up and eyed him.

Matt rubbed his chin in thought. "We do have chocolate chip."

"Mommy loves ice cream." Faith closed her eyes with a yawn.

"We've had a busy day. Let's get some rest. I'll take the meal out when it's done."

He slowly walked to her bedroom and put Faith in bed. He pulled the comforter around her and kissed her cheek. "Since we bought this fine chair," He pointed to the seat a few steps from the bed. "Why don't I sit in here with you?" Matt lowered himself in the comfortable padded cushion. "I'll write while you sleep."

"Are you making a new book?" She yawned again.

"I am."

"Good night Daddy." She closed her eyes.

Matt quickly got his laptop and hurried back to Faith's room. He opened his work in progress. Faith coughed and he glanced her way, determined that she would rest better tonight.

He planned to write the first two chapters sitting in her chair, beside her bed.

He clicked his bookmarker and read Ecclesiastes 3:2 "A time to be born, and a time to die; a time to plant, and a time to pluck up that which is planted." He typed the scenario for his main character in Twenty-Eight Seasons. He wet his lips while the words flowed from his mind to his fingers already anticipating the path of redemption his book would take.

He stopped writing and looked across the room at his little girl curled up on her side, in peaceful sleep. He analyzed the past and events that brought him to this day. Just like his life, his new genre would take getting used to, for him and for his readers. Quietly, he huffed. *Many of my currant fans won't read clean novels, but there's a whole new world of book-lovers out there.* He looked down at his computer, his fingers tapped on the keys. Like the smell of his mom's brownies, which always called him toward the kitchen, his make-believe creation beckoned him along.

• • ❧ • •

THE CELL PHONE BUZZED. Lucinda noted her friend's number.

"Hi. How's your day been?"

"Good, except for the baby is cutting a tooth." Cynthia's sentence came slow.

"Goodness, I know that's a challenge. I remember Faith's teething battles."

"Speaking of Faith how is everything going now that she knows Matt is her father?"

"Better than I imagined." Lucinda put her paper towels away and sat on her bar stool. "She's with him right now."

"That's good." Cynthia hesitated, "isn't it?"

"Yes, Faith needs to get to know her father, but I miss my little girl."

"I understand. Have you and Matt talked about it?"

"We have. Matt says he doesn't want to take her from me."

"There you go. Put it into God's hands, all will work out."

"I know you're right." Lucinda sighed, "But it's difficult sometimes."

"It is. We're all human and don't like waiting for things to happen." She chuckled. "Jesus has this."

"He does. I hope He watches after us tomorrow. Matt's bringing Faith to church. I can only guess the comments that will be made."

"Oh my!" Her friend suddenly picked up pace with her words. "Remember how things were when you first started going to church? Still, you diplomatically handled all their questions about being a single mother."

"Yeah, I recall." Lucinda swung her foot as she spoke. "Things would have been easier, If I just lied and said my husband was dead. I knew I wouldn't feel comfortable telling such an exaggeration."

"You only said that it was you and her, and that, right now her father wasn't in the picture. Just be discreet like you were before. The only thing that matters is that you're God's child."

"You're right." Lucinda nodded, "It would be so easy to tell folks that she is adopted, but Matt and I agreed that we need to wait. Finding her father has been a big enough change for Faith."

"I'll back you up tomorrow. Everyone will probably think you and Matt have a history but it'll be okay. The Lord knows."

"Thanks, Cynthia. You've probably made sleep much easier tonight."

Lucinda and Cynthia went on to chat about different medications to soothe a baby's sore gums. Forty minutes later, Lucinda bid her friend a good-bye and strolled to her room. Ugly scenarios of the things she might face in church the next morning filled her mind.

CHAPTER SIXTEEN

Sunday morning Lucinda watched Matt and Faith pull into the church lot. Several members turned their heads as he parked his shiny red luxury car. Matt went around to the backseat. Seconds later, Faith was out of her seat looking around. "Where's Mommy?"

"Here she comes." Matt pointed to Lucinda, hustling toward them.

"Honey?" She circled Faith in her arms.

"Hi Mommy." Faith hugged her.

"Have you had fun at Daddy's?"

"Uh-huh." Faith nodded. "Wait until you see my dollhouse."

"Must be something. That's all she's talked about." Lucinda looked at Matt.

"I picked it up in Washington at a toy store. It's a castle for a Barbie. When I saw it, I could see her playing." Matt touched Lucinda's arm. "She's welcome to take it home, to your house."

"Thanks, Matt. Are you ready for this?" She gestured toward the worship center.

"All set. Our child is what is important, everyone else will understand in time."

"I hope you're right." She glimpsed at Faith. "Let's go.

They walked into the foyer. Pastor Lamoure stood greeting the congregation. He welcomed them and nodded at Matt.

"Matt, it's wonderful to have you with us," The pastor's face spread with a toothy grin, "Lucinda and Faith, lovely as always."

"Thank you." Lucinda had her hand on Faith's shoulder.

"Pastor, did you get your battery replaced?" Matt stepped aside to let another man pass.

"I did. I'm trouble free now. Car wise, that is. We all have situations that ruffle our feathers, as my dad used to say. God has us under His watchful eye though."

"You're right, Pastor." Matt leaned back on his heel. "I've made peace, but I'm sure I'll still have a few feathers to smooth along the way."

Pastor Lamoure chuckled, "I'm sure."

"We'd better find a seat." Matt glanced around.

Lucinda led the way as Faith and Matt followed. He nodded in greeting as people spoke, and shook hands while they made their way to a pew and found a seat. Joan Burr extended her pace, and headed in their direction.

Lucinda leaned close to Matt and whispered. "Oh no."

"My goodness I'm glad to see you again." Joan addressed Matt. "I thought you'd gone for good. After all, you're one of those big time authors?" She reached out and touched his hand, which rested on the top of the bench. "When you left town, I realized why you looked so familiar. I've seen your novels in the bookstore."

"It looks like I'm going to make Black Mountain home for a while." Matt laid his Bible on the pew.

"Daddy is staying close to me." Faith interjected.

"Daddy?" Joan's eyes grew into saucers. She looked from Matt to Lucinda. "Well, this is certainly a surprise. Lucinda, why didn't you tell us he was Faith's father?"

"I... Um..." Lucinda swallowed what she was sure must be a goose egg. "I didn't feel like it was the right time."

"Humph," She grimaced. "Would appear it was something you couldn't avoid."

Lucinda's pasty complexion met Matt. He glanced her way and then addressed Joan. "We erred on the side of caution for Faith's sake. A child isn't responsible for an adult's short-comings." One of his crowd-pleasing smiles flourished. "I can tell that you're a wonderful lady of discretion, and also you're very lovely today."

"Gracious," Joan chuckled and touched her hair. Her cheeks wrinkled from appreciation. "You're an insightful man."

Lucinda watched Matt work his charm. She could almost see Joan puddle onto the floor. She pressed her mouth tight to keep from grinning.

An announcement interrupted the conversation. Matt grinned at Joan one more time. "I think the service is beginning. Have a wonderful day."

Lucinda leaned toward Matt and eyed Joan as the woman ambled away. "Don't, for a minute, think you can pull that on me."

"What do you mean?" The corners of his eyes crinkled and he lifted his brow.

"I'll not fall for your manly charms. Mr. Blake." She pretended indifference, but couldn't stop her mouth from turning up from amusement. Lucinda looked at the altar. She planned to enjoy a day in worship. When morning service was over, they gathered Faith and quietly left.

● ● ✑ ● ●

"WELCOME TO MY HUMBLE abode." Matt held the door for Lucinda as she entered the living room.

She cast an eye over the space. "You have a nice place."

"Mommy, come see my room." Faith tugged on the tail of her coat as she removed it.

"Go. I have a salad to toss." Matt took her jacket and hung it in the coat closet.

Later, Matt walked to Faith's room and found Lucinda sitting with crossed legs, on the floor. Their daughter was rearranging the dollhouse furniture.

"Lunch is served, my ladies."

"Come on honey." Lucinda waited for Faith to stand her doll's make up dresser in place.

In the dining room, Matt pulled the chair out for Lucinda, and helped Faith be seated before he took his place at the table.

"Baked spaghetti." Lucinda looked at the meal and grinned.

"It's your favorite, Mommy."

"It's one of my indulgences."

"Faith said you'd be pleased." Matt touched her hand. "Would you like to bless the meal?"

"I can." She grinned, "Heavenly Father, thanks for this wonderful lunch. Bless us all and be with Matt in his new writing endeavor. Amen"

"Amen." Matt repeated. "Thank you for lifting up my new venture to the Lord."

"You're welcome. I'm looking forward to reading your next story." She spooned a serving of pasta for her and Faith. "I liked the sermon today. Pastor Lamoure made some good points as he ministered on the Lord's guidance."

Matt handed his daughter a slice of bread. "I never gave it much thought before. But it does make sense to seek God's Holy word, before decisions are made." He passed a French roll to Lucinda.

"Yes, I'll remember what he said for a long time. Trust, ask and wait on God." She took a bite, and thought about the message.

"I need to reread Psalms." He lifted his glass.

"Psalms 32:8 is one of my favorites. "I will instruct you and teach you in the way you should go; I will counsel you with my eye upon you.'"

"Is Jesus like a Mommy and Daddy?" Faith's question had both of them eyeing her.

"We're all God's children." Lucinda grinned. "Age doesn't matter. The Lord tells us right from wrong, if we listen."

"Even big people need to be told what to do!" Faith turned to Matt.

"Sometimes, adults do things that aren't right, but the Bible teaches all of us." Matt cupped his hands in his lap. Amazed at how easy speaking about the Holy Word had become.

They finished the meal. Matt asked about dessert. "Faith says you enjoy ice cream. I have chocolate chip." He dipped out a small bowl for Faith.

"Maybe later," Lucinda paid attention to her daughter as she took delight in her sweet treat. While Faith ate, they chatted about Christmas.

"Are you putting up a tree?" Lucinda asked.

"I guess I will. I normally have a small one on my desktop. This year, I have a reason for a bigger celebration." He glanced at Faith as she gulped the last of her melted ice cream.

"Faith honey, don't do that, it's not polite." Lucinda shook her head.

"It's a sign of deliciousness." Matt chuckled. "Princess, will you go play for a while? I want to talk to Mommy."

"Uh-huh." She scooted off her chair and headed to her room.

"I hope you don't mind. I need to see how you feel about something before I mention it to Faith."

"Sure." Lucinda laid her arms on the table.

"You recall me telling you that I spoke with my parents." Matt saw her nod. "They want to meet Faith. I would like your blessing to take her to visit them next week, before the holidays."

"I can't dream of a Christmas without her." Lucinda shook her head. "Didn't you say they live in Colorado?"

"Denver. I have a friend with a single-pilot business jet." Matt kept eye contact as he explained. "He tells me that he can go on Tuesday. We'll be back by Friday. I hope that you'll agree. Mom just wants to meet her granddaughter."

"I can sympathize with her." She touched the tips of her fingers together. "This is hard. I know Faith's your daughter and needs to have you in her life, but it's been me and her." She pushed her hair aside. "Now, all of a sudden I'm sharing her." She closed her eyes for a second and sighed. "I'm sorry. I'm not very good at this."

"It's a big change for all of us, Faith included. I promise I'll always try to keep in mind that you're the one who has made Faith the wonderful little girl she is." Matt massaged her wrist. Time froze. He fell into orbs of soft blue and licked his lips, remembering the last time they kissed. Without pulling his hand from hers, he stood and tenderly nudged her to her feet.

"I thought my life was complete, until I came back here." He looked down at her and closed the inches between them until their lips touched. He moved in rhythm with her as she responded to his kiss.

Suddenly she pulled away. "Please, I'm confused enough without this." She touched her lips.

"There's nothing to be puzzled about. Knowing who Faith is doesn't change the fact that I'm attracted to you, in many ways." He rubbed her cheek with the back of his hand. His fingers outlined her mouth.

"This is too fast." She took another step back. "I need to get accustomed to you as Faith's father. For now, that's all I can handle."

"Very well." He nodded. "Nevertheless, I do want us to get to know each other better."

"Maybe." He noticed Lucinda turned her head toward the sound of little feet.

"Mommy, you and daddy talking?"

"We've finished." She bent down and hugged the child.

"Lucinda, we didn't get around to discussing the plans." Matt reminded.

"I'll be worried, but I've got to get used to that too." She attempted a smile. "Keep her safe."

"Mommy, why you gonna worry?"

"Honey, you and Daddy are going on a trip to see your grandma."

"When?" She looked up at Matt.

"The day after tomorrow we'll ride on a plane. Are you okay with that?"

"Yippee." Her head bobbed up and down, she clasped her hands together. "Mommy coming?"

"Not this time. You'll be fine." Lucinda lifted the right side of her mouth in a tentative unsure grin.

"We'll only be gone a couple days." Matt watched them, as if a breeze blew through the kitchen, a feeling of uncertainty milled around. At that point, he realized the magnitude of the situation. The Wise family also changed, the day he pulled into Lucinda's driveway. "Faith, do you want to go home with Mommy? I'll come pick you up early Tuesday morning to visit grandma."

"Yeah." Her mouth spread in pleasure.

• • ❧ • •

MATT PICKED UP SEVERAL of Faith's toys and tossed them in the basket he designated for her playthings. He gathered a miniature hair dryer and marveled at the details of the beauty apparatus. With his daughter's room de-cluttered, he pulled her door shut, and went to the living room. His hand pressed the screen on his cell.

"Lucinda, I was making sure you got home safely."

"We're here." A low laugh met his ear. "We've made the three mile trip from town many times."

"I'm sorry. I know you're quite competent."

"It's fine. You mean well."

"Tell Faith good night for me." Matt leaned back on the sofa.

"I will. She's playing with her gerbil."

"Good night, Lucinda."

"Night."

He ended the call and tossed the phone on the cushion beside him. "Changes." He spoke the word aloud. The challenges he felt from his bout of writer's block didn't compare to the compromises his life was taking on now. He recalled the first time Lucinda had spoken about the verses in Ecclesiastes. "To everything there is a season." He quoted part of verse three, chapter one. This year was definitely his season for adjustments.

He put his head in his hands, seeking strength. "Holy Father, lead the way. Guide me to do the right things. I'm not as sure, as I pretend."

CHAPTER SEVENTEEN

Matt arrived at Lucinda's before sunrise. She greeted him, yawned and pointed to the hot coffee. "Make yourself at home. Cups are in the cupboard over the pot. Faith's almost ready." She moved close to Matt and lowered her voice. "I don't mind telling you, I'm a little worried about this flight. She's never been on a airplane."

"I promise you, that my friend is a very knowledgeable pilot. She'll be safe." He rubbed her arm. "Lucinda, I would lay my life down to protect her."

"I will be praying for you both."

"Thanks." He grinned as she hastened toward the child's room. While he waited, he poured a mug of the morning brew.

As Matt loaded the car with his daughter's suitcase he momentarily looked at Lucinda and Faith saying their goodbyes. He shut the trunk. "May I see your phone?" She handed him her cell and moved her lip sideways in question.

He pressed some numbers. "You can contact Mom if you get worried. I tagged it as Grandmother Blake." He kissed her on the cheek, got inside his car and pulled out, heading to the small airstrip.

Twenty minutes passed and he pulled in the garage, adjacent to his friend's private jet. They boarded the plane. He buckled Faith in the seat beside him and hugged her. "This will be fun. I put you in the window seat, so you can see the clouds."

Awaiting take-off, his mind went back to the simple kiss he'd gave Lucinda on the cheek. He didn't miss the slight tilt of her head. *How would she react if I held her in my arms the way I really want to?*

"Daddy." Faith tugged on his shirt. "Look!" She motioned toward a cloud. "It looks like a big pillow." She giggled as her voice rose from the excitement.

During the short flight to Colorado, Matt pointed landmarks out to Faith. The child eagerly examined the mountainous peaks and the splendor below.

"Buckle-up, we're approaching the Denver airstrip." Matt patted Faith on the shoulder as his friend's announcement filled the space.

. . ❧ . .

MATT EXITED THE RENTAL car and helped Faith from her seat. His parents open their door. He bent down to his daughter. "That's Grandma and Grandpa. They're excited to have you for their granddaughter."

His mom hurried down the sidewalk. "Matt, it's so good to see you." She kissed his cheek, stepped back and cradled her hands together. "This must be Faith."

"Yes Ma'am." Faith put her finger in her mouth.

"Aren't you a cutie?" Mom leaned down and hugged the child. "I want you to call me Grandma."

"And I'm your grandpa." Dad's jovial voice added as he stepped closer to Faith. "It's wonderful to have you in the family." He shook her hand and chuckled. "Grandma is right. You're a pretty little lady."

"Thank you." Faith grinned.

"Let's go inside everyone." Dad hugged Matt and picked up a suitcase.

Matt followed his family and escorted his daughter into the house.

"I know you're exhausted from your trip." Mom put everyone's coat away and sat beside Faith.

"I was watching the clouds." Faith made a circle with her arms. "Big and fluffy."

"The horizon is beautiful." Mom grinned at the child.

"If you're not tired we can bake cookies while Daddy and Grandpa talk."

"Okay." Faith slid off the sofa.

Matt glanced after them while they strolled into the kitchen. "Excuse me, Dad. I need to make a phone call." He pressed Lucinda's number.

"Matt, I was nervously waiting for your call."

"You can relax. All went well. Faith enjoyed her first plane ride."

"I'm glad. What's she doing?"

"She's in the kitchen with Mom, baking cookies." Matt glanced toward the doorway.

"I won't disturb her. She needs to get to know your mother."

"Thanks. I'll let her talk to you before bedtime." Matt rubbed his neck. "You're a special lady."

"That's nice of you to say. Thank you again, for calling."

Matt laid his phone down and eyed his father. "I suppose you have a hundred questions."

"Mom and I talked about your situation. Son, we've all been young." Walter Blake shook his head. "Back then, we knew you and Sonya were in love. You were eighteen, raised in church. Parents can only hope and pray that some of the teachings stick. That being said, I'm amazed with this story. It's a testimony of how God can place others in our paths at the right time." Dad rubbed his mouth. "I'm glad that Lucinda Wise befriended Sonya."

"Me too, Lucinda is a wonderful mother. I think back and realize I didn't love Sonya the way I thought. If I had I don't believe I'd have moved." Matt eyed his dad. "Knowing about Faith makes me speculate about how things would've been if I stayed in Black Mountain."

"Hum." Dad turned and faced Matt. "You remember the verse in Philippians 3:13, that says, 'Brethren, I count not myself to have apprehended: but [this] one thing [I do], forgetting those things which are behind, and reaching forth unto those things which are before.'" Dad patted Matt's shoulder. "Forgiveness is ours. All Jesus wants is for us to dedicate ourselves to living by his teachings and to do good things for His glory."

"I know. Dad, I've repented. I've even started to write more uplifting novels."

Matt continued to bring his dad up to speed with all the changes he had accepted since learning he was a father. When he finished outlining his personal writing dilemma, he spoke more about Lucinda.

"It sounds as if you like her in more ways than just a mother for your child." Dad watched his son.

As if he was under a magnifying glass, Matt turned his head away from his dad's comment, "Even before I knew about

Faith, I wanted to go out with Lucinda and get to know her better."

"So what's stopping you? She sounds like a good Christian woman."

"She is." Matt pressed his lips tight and paused. "I've asked her out. She hasn't agreed to go. It seems that since I found out about Faith she's backed away."

"Women are a wonder sometimes. If I've learned anything from being married to your mother all these years, it's that, they will think a situation to death. Mom takes days to pick out a new paint color. I'll choose the first neutral tone I see, and not give it a second thought." Dad chuckled. "They all look taupe or pale blue to me, but I think your mom knows every tone by name."

Dad stood and poked at the log in the fireplace. "I'm sure Lucinda's head is spinning with what if's. Perhaps, she thinks that if anything were to develop between you two, it would be because of the child. Tell her how you feel. You have to be straight forward."

He watched Dad stir the flame. *Doesn't Lucinda realize that I care for her?*

• • ❧ • •

"WILL YOU FEEL SAFE in the guest room? I can rest in here with you. Grandma has a sleeping bag."

"It's okay, Daddy." Faith held out her arms to hug him.

Matt inhaled the scent of her freshly washed hair and remembered Mom called the aroma Lavender pedals. It smelt like bubble gum to him. He pulled the quilt over his daughter.

"Grandma, let you use her bath milk."

"Uh-huh. She told me the story of baby Jesus' birth. Mommy and me read it every year. I didn't tell Grandma."

"Grandma enjoys Christmas. Her favorite part is celebrating Jesus' birth."

"Mommy says that too." She turned on her side to face him. "Daddy, you can come and live with me and mommy. I know you like her. I saw you kiss."

"Princess." He bided for time. *What do I say?* "I care for mommy very much, but she needs time to adjust to me being in your life."

"I was mixed up when Mommy told me you were my daddy. Why did you stay away?"

Matt looked at Faith. Her mouth wiggled to one side. He'd learned to recognize that as a sign, she was unsure about the answer she'd receive. "That's a hard question for me to answer right now. I promise that one day when you're older, I'll tell you the whole story. Please, understand that I came into your life as soon as I could. I love you very much." Her hesitant expression turned into a smile. "Get some sleep. Tomorrow will be a long day. I think Grandma, and Grandpa wants you to go to a tree farm with them, and pick out the tree."

"Oh boy." She clapped. "Christmas tree."

"Good night." He stood and waited to see what she'd do.

"Daddy, I'm okay. Grandma says she's right here, on the other side." She touched the wall.

"You're becoming a big girl." He grinned and took his phone from his pocket. "I'll call Mommy. You can say goodnight."

When Matt heard the rings he handed the cell to Faith and walked over to the window to close the blind. Faith told

Lucinda about making cookies and their plans to go shopping. He turned, as his daughter was ending the call.

"Nighty-night Mommy. I luv you." She gave him the phone. He listened to silence on the cell. "I guess Mommy's hung up. "Rest well."

After enjoying a cup of cocoa with his parents, he retired to the room his dad called the office. Mom had dressed the pull out couch with a soft comforter and large pillow. Matt slipped on his jogging pants, grabbed his laptop and crawled under the cover. He booted up and started to type, then stopped. Faith's questions frosted over any ideas he had about working on his novel. He closed the lid to his computer. "Lord, thanks for placing the words in my mouth to give that wonderful little girl a response to satisfy her until she's older."

He reached for his phone and pushed Lucinda's number. "Hi. Did I wake you?" He listened to her yawn.

"No. I was lying here thinking about our daughter."

"I just wanted you to know that I'm grateful we both can be part of Faith's life."

"It's the right thing to do. I love her, and she needs her father." She paused. "Faith also should have a good relationship with her grandparents."

"I'm not as bull headed as you may think. I recognize that this is a burden for you." Matt listened to the silence for a second.

"It's a new path." She paused. "Part of those changes we humans must face."

"I hadn't thought of it like that. Lucinda, I hope you won't think of me as an unwelcomed modification. I really do care for you." Some of what his Dad said played in his mind. He added.

"Faith doesn't have a thing to do with my attraction toward you. You're beautiful, smart and a good person. I'd have to be nuts not to want to smother you with kisses and hold you in my arms."

"I'm flattered. Where did all that come from?"

"I'm only putting it out there, in case you wondered about ulterior motives."

"Thanks for clarifying." She laughed. "I don't mean to change the subject. I like to hear those flowered words, but how is Faith doing on her adventure?"

Matt told Lucinda about the events at the Blake household. He highlighted the homemade cookie episode and chuckled. "You should have seen her and Mom, they had flour everywhere. Mom made Faith a warm bath with lots of bubbles."

"I know she enjoyed that." She cleared her throat. "Matt, thank you for calling."

"You're welcome. I'll let Faith tell you about the tree they pick out tomorrow."

"I'll look forward to it."

Before he ended the call, Lucinda's next words rushed forth. "You're the first man I've enjoyed spending time around, and having conversations with, in a long while."

"Thank you." He lowered his voice, "Good night, beautiful."

• • ❧ • •

COLORFUL LIGHTS ON the tree flickered, as if they were playing a melody. Matt stood and watched as Faith hung the last Christmas ball on a branch.

"Okay?" She looked at the adults.

"Perfect." Grandma placed her hand on Faith's back. "This tree will stay just the way you've decorated it, until Santa comes." She stepped back and eyed the garland.

"If Daddy lets me, I'll call you Christmas." Faith grinned.

"Of course you can." Matt interjected. "You may talk to Grandma anytime. Mommy has her number too."

"And I look forward to meeting your Mommy." Grandma picked up a box that held leftover ornaments.

Matt eyed several empty containers and addressed his parents. "I'll get Faith settled and give you a hand putting these away."

"Good night." Faith hugged Grandma and gave Grandpa a bear hug.

"You're a strong little lady, aren't you?" Grandpa grinned.

• • ❧ • •

THE NEXT MORNING THE Blake family had a big breakfast. Matt passed a muffin to Faith.

"I hope you enjoy the blueberry kind." Grandma waited for her to sample the morning treat.

"Yummy." Faith took another bite. "I like pumpkin too."

"That's good to know. I have some wonderful pumpkin recipes. The next time you visit we'll prepare a special indulgence."

"Mommy makes pumpkin pies. We grow lots of 'em."

Grandma leaned toward Faith. "One day I'd like to see your pumpkin patch."

After breakfast, Matt carried his tote and Faith's luggage into the living room. He placed them by the door.

"I'm glad to see you're finding your place in the world." Dad pulled him close for a quick hug.

"I thought that I'd discovered it years ago." Matt grinned.

"Son, money and fame aren't what make you a winner. Nor, does it define a person's worth, or what's in their heart."

"I know that now. As usual, Dad you're right." Matt looked down the hallway when he heard footsteps.

"She's ready." Grandma announced, and then went to the tree and retrieved presents. "Before you go I have early Christmas gifts."

"Oh boy." Faith ran over to Grandma.

"Mom, you can mail them." Matt moved closer.

"Nonsense. Why can't she have her gifts now?"

"Daddy, please." Faith shifted her feet.

"Go ahead." Matt sat on the edge of the sofa while his daughter opened two gifts.

"It's a set of colored pencils." Grandma nodded as Faith held out the art set. "Dad told me how much you enjoy sketching." Grandma showed the child how to close the art kit so she could carry it by the handle.

Matt grinned at his daughter as she picked up the next gift. She tore into snowman paper to uncover a child's learning pad.

"Mom, you and Dad are spoiling her already." He shook his head.

"We only wanted to get her something to help her. She'll be going to school soon. The sales lady said this is the best device for kids' five to nine." Dad gathered the ripped Christmas wrap.

"I've heard about them." Matt recalled seeing advertising that claimed to enhance a child's desire for knowledge.

He gave his parents time to enjoy Faith's reaction to her new toys. Thirty minutes later he stood. "I hate to say this. If we don't go we'll be late." He looked at his daughter. "Mommy will be wondering where we are."

 • • ᴐᏇᴐ • •

WHEN THEY ARRIVED BACK in North Carolina, and left the airport, darkness had ascended. Matt looked up at the glimmer which illuminated the sky, from the numerous stars. The twinkles reminded him of the Christmas tree at his mom's house. It was nice to visit. Still, he breathed relief at being home. He pulled beside Lucinda's house, turned off the car engine, and heard Faith scoot from the car seat. She ran to the door, while he was still getting out.

"Honey, I'm glad you're home." Lucinda grabbed her daughter in a hug.

"Me too Mommy," Faith looked back at Matt. "Daddy, hurry I want to show Mommy what Grandma and Grandpa got me for Christmas."

"Christmas?" Lucinda lifted her brow.

"They wanted to give out gifts before we left." Matt gathered his daughter's suitcase and presents from the car.

"Come inside," Lucinda laughed, while she held the door. "You have your hands full."

"Here, Princess." He handed his daughter her items.

"I have a fresh pot of coffee if you'd like." Lucinda motioned to the counter and took the art set Faith handed her.

Matt went to the coffee pot. He leaned against the counter and listened to Faith explain her gifts to Lucinda. He sipped the warm java while the child highlighted the details of her trip to her mother. Two cups of coffee later, Lucinda interrupted Faith.

"Honey, let's save the rest for tomorrow. You look exhausted." She pushed a loose strand of hair from Faith's face. "Are you tired?"

"I guess." Faith yawned.

"Tell Daddy good night. We'll get you in bed."

"Night Daddy." Faith rushed to circle her arms around his neck. She kissed him on the cheek.

"Rest well, Princess." Matt returned the hug.

"When will I stay at your house again?"

Matt glanced at Lucinda. She nodded.

"Mi casa es su casa." He took hold of Faith's pint size fingers.

"Huh?" Faith's mouth rounded in surprise.

"It means my house is your house. You can come anytime that Mommy says it's okay." He turned his attention to Lucinda. "If possible every other weekend, maybe sometimes during the week, if she wants."

"Faith can." Lucinda stepped forward, "But now it's time for bed." She turned and addressed Matt. "I'll be right back, if you want to stay for a bit, make yourself at home."

Matt strolled into the living room and sat down. He noticed fifteen minutes had passed before Lucinda joined him.

"She's excited about the trip." She sat next to him on the sofa.

"Thanks for letting her go. She had a good time. So did my parents." He reached for Lucinda's hand. "They want to meet you too. Dad says that he believes God placed you in the right spot at the perfect time."

"I've often thought that." She looked at their fingers entwined. "I realize you can take Faith anywhere you wish. You have every right, but thanks for understanding." She moved her finger across the top of his hand.

"You're her mother and always will be. It's what Sonya wanted. I want that too." He tried to be discreet while he moved closer.

"Have you given any thought to us going out?" Matt turned her head toward him and became lost in her eyes. Not waiting for an answer he soaked in the softness of her lips, lightly tasting them. A breath later, he increased his embrace to capture every inch of her mouth before he slowly backed away. "I want..." His eyes lingered on her face. "I appreciate that our situation is unique. I believe that we're way beyond being attracted to each other." He toyed with her hair.

"Yes." She ran her finger over his cheek and let out an uneven breath. "I'll see if Cynthia's niece can babysit one evening." Lucinda sighed, and then smiled. "I can't deny that I'm attracted to you." She moved from the sofa suddenly unsure. "It's been a while since I've felt this way about anyone. I need to take things slow."

"I won't pressure you." He stood, walked to her side, tilted her head toward him and circled her in his arms for a hug. "Good night beautiful."

CHAPTER EIGHTEEN

Lucinda headed to the door to welcome Matt. "Come in. I'll get my coat." As she stepped into the next room rushing footsteps greeted him.

"Daddy." Faith ran into his arms. "You're taking Mommy to a movie. Is it the one we seen?"

"No. It's a different one, Princess." He grinned at his daughter as she planted a smooch on his cheek.

"Mommy says I can stay with you this weekend."

"Wonderful. I'll pick you up in the morning."

"Okay." She slid from his grasp. "I luv you."

"I love you too." Matt hugged her good-bye.

. . ⚘ . .

LUCINDA STROLLED INTO the lobby of the theater. Matt held the door to the entertainment area. "I enjoyed our meal together." He reached for her hand.

"I did too." She tried to ignore the warm bubbly feeling his touch created. "I'd forgotten how much I liked a good steak. I don't eat it much because Faith's doesn't care for red meat and she definitely doesn't like T-bone."

"She hasn't been exposed to my grilling talents yet. Wait until spring." Matt chuckled. "I'll prepare one of the small thin tenderloins for her." He nodded as if the matter was solved.

Lucinda looked toward the hall, which led to various rooms. "Which theater is airing that new romantic suspense?"

"The one nearest the door, I already have tickets. We can go find our seats."

They entered the darkened area, Lucinda eyed one corner, and then another. "Where would you like to sit?"

As long as it's not in the first two rows I'm fine." He stepped to the side. "Let's take these seats." He scooted between rows, to the left of the aisle.

"This is the last set of chairs." Lucinda followed.

"Yeah." Matt glanced back. "We can sit against the wall and pretend we're teenagers' again."

"Awesome." She giggled.

As the last hour winded down Lucinda leaned close to Matt, immersed in the plot. She inwardly cheered on the main character as he climbed into an abandoned building. Her breath caught when the scene changed and the actor lifted his love from a smoldering flame, just in time to save her. The couple kissed as the end approached.

Lucinda turned her head toward him when Matt touched her chin. "I'd do that for you."

"You would?" She felt her cheeks grow warm and met his stare, only hazily aware of the people who were leaving the theater.

"I would risk my life to pull you from danger."

Lucinda gave into her longing to enjoy his kiss, not caring that they were in a public setting. Seconds passed, before she backed away. "We should go. They'll run us out." She pressed her lips together and grinned as he put a strand of her hair behind her ear.

. . ❧ . .

THE NEXT MORNING LUCINDA opened the door. "Faith's not ready yet. I made pancakes, want one?"

"No." Matt rubbed his hands together. "I want about three." He lifted his brow. "If it's okay."

"Sure." Lucinda laughed, and added another place setting. "I'll get Faith. We can enjoy breakfast."

"Daddy?" Faith ran into the kitchen. "Mommy says you're eating with us."

"I am. I'm starved for pancakes."

"Mommy makes the bestest." Faith scooted onto her chair.

With the meal blessed, Lucinda gave Faith her serving and handed the plate of hotcakes to Matt. She snickered as he took a pancake, and then went back for more.

"Would you like maple syrup?" She passed the bottle and eyed him as he enjoyed the dish. *What would it be like to wake up beside him, and cook for him every day?* When the notion crossed in her mind, she shook her head.

"What?" Matt grinned and swallowed. "I have a good appetite.

"I see that." She turned her attention to her plate.

The trio ate in silence. When breakfast was over Lucinda loaded the dishwasher and listened to Matt and Faith chatting in the next room. She walked into the living room to see Matt helping her daughter with her coat.

"You have fun at Daddy's. Be a good girl."

"I will." The child grabbed her stuffed bear. "Will the tree be up when I get home?"

"Yes and I think a few gifts will be under it too." Lucinda smiled at her five year old.

"Oh boy." Faith clapped.

"You can't be shaking the presents this year." She went to the car with Matt and Faith and adjusted her daughter's booster seat. "Ready." Lucinda shut the child's door.

"I'm going to miss you." Matt hugged Lucinda.

"Me, or my cooking?" She laughed.

"You certainly, but Faith's right, you're a wonderful cook."

"Anyone can make pancakes." She pictured their last kiss and clasped her hands together to keep from reaching out to him.

"Not true, my lady. The last time I tried to make hot cakes I could have used them as flying saucers." He chuckled and ran his hand over her cheek. "If you get lonely you know where we'll be."

"Thanks, but I have a Christmas tree to pull out and decorate."

"I figured you'd wait for Faith to help."

"She does like to lend a hand, but it's faster with me doing it by myself." She grinned. "Usually we put it up a week before Christmas, but her visit with your parents jump-started her holiday. She wants it early."

"Sorry." Matt lowered his head as if he was ashamed. "It's my fault."

"All's good." She quickly ran her hand through a few strands of his hair.

"The last months of this year are special for Faith. She's been united with her father and her grandparents."

"I know how she feels. It's been wonderful. I have a daughter, a new path in writing, a rededication with Jesus Christ, and I have you in my life." He grinned. "I believe God guided me to find my place, and my real treasures. Like Dad says, a person's worth is more than a portfolio."

"Daddy, ready?" Faith raised her voice so they could hear her through the car window. "I want to play with my dollhouse."

"I better go." Matt caressed Lucinda's face with a light kiss. "Remember, we're only a few miles away."

Lucinda watched Matt and Faith turn out of the driveway. She went back into the house and cleaned the kitchen. With her chores finished, she climbed the stairs to the attic and manhandled a long box with a picture of a Christmas tree to the living room. A couple trips later, she had cartons of holiday ornaments laid out.

The evening wore on as Lucinda decorated for the holiday. She put the last snow globe ball on the tree and gathered a couple of presents she'd stashed. Her cell phone buzzed.

"Hi." Cynthia's chipper voice greeted Lucinda. "You busy?"

"Not now. I just finished putting up the tree."

"James put up ours. He's overjoyed about our first Christmas with the baby."

"I'll bet he spoils that cutie and probably buys out the store." Lucinda let out a short laugh and pulled the ottoman close to the tree. "Faith's little trip to her grandparents has her counting away the days."

"Are you..." Cynthia paused. "Okay with everything that's going on?"

"I am." She added a tree skirt and placed a couple gifts. "It's funny. I'm more at ease with Matt being Faith's father than I am with the idea of a relationship with the man."

"Lucinda, I know you really like him. From what you tell me he cares for you, if the reason isn't the fact that he's Faith's father, then why the apprehension?"

"I've asked myself the same thing." She rose from her seat. "At least, Matt and I have started dating."

"It's about time."

"What?" Lucinda frowned. "Why do you say it like that?"

"You seem to be pushing him away from falling in love with you."

"Humph." Lucinda grunted. "No, I haven't. I don't see it like that."

"Well, girlfriend, open your eyes. He's the first man you've been interested in since you've moved to town. Still, you've made one excuse after another not to spend time with him."

Lucinda gnawed on her lip and deliberated her friend's words. "I didn't realize, but you could be right. I suppose I should pray about it. Maybe, I'm scared that it won't last. Faith could get hurt."

"He will always be Faith's father. You know, there are no guarantees in life. All we can do is walk with the Lord and have confidence in His word." She let out a breath. "You have to stop being scared of living."

"I'm not anxious about things."

"Really?" Lucinda grinned at Cynthia's tone. She'd witnessed her say that word many times, and pictured the way she rounded her mouth with the question. "What's that reaction for?"

"Like I said, since you've lived here you've led a sheltered life."

"I've not!" Lucinda's voice lifted. "I have my pumpkin farm and my accounting career. I stay busy and active. I also volunteer for church functions."

"You do." Cynthia's tone was flat. "And you've turned down countless dinner invitations from nice, God-fearing men. Need I remind you about Ray? He has a good career, he's handsome, and not to mention, kind. I know of at least a dozen times he approached you for a date. That tells me you're afraid to move past the secure life you've built with Faith."

"I can't talk about this anymore." Lucinda rubbed her arm as if the truth of her friend's words had poked her.

"I'm sorry for being matter-of-fact. I only want you to open your eyes. Stop putting yourself in a bubble."

"I'll think about it." She picked up a pack of icicles. "I'll chat later. I have one more thing to add to the tree."

"Okay, girl friend. Goodbye."

Sundown layered Black Mountain with a foggy haze. Lucinda gazed from her window, to the scripture she was reading. 'Be of good courage, and he shall strengthen your heart, all ye that hope in the LORD.' She let the pages fall, while the meaning of the verse in Psalms tugged at her with questions. Lucinda laid the Bible on the side table and went to freshen up.

An hour later, she yawned and turned off her lamp. Parts of the scripture from God's Holy Word still lingered. *Good courage.* She closed her eyes and prayed. "Heavenly Father, help me to have the sureness to move forward with my life. Guide me in the path I should walk. Amen."

She bunched up her pillow and snuggled into the soft down. Like a stampede, her discussion with Cynthia trampled into her night. *Lord, why have I been scared to get involved in a relationship?*

CHAPTER NINETEEN

Matt stood beside Faith and knocked. The sound of Lucinda's footsteps increased and the door swung wide.

"Come in."

"Mickey missed me." Faith passed Matt and hurried inside to see her gerbil.

"Did Faith behave?" Lucinda stepped back to give him space to enter.

"She's a sweetie. One time she was a bit too insistent on eating her dessert before dinner. I had to negotiate with her. She realized she didn't want to lose play time on her learning tablet." He shrugged. "All worked out."

"It sounds like you're learning to be longsuffering." She smiled.

"Perhaps, being a father has softened me."

"Join us." Lucinda led the way.

"Daddy, look at the tree." Faith jumped in surprise. "Pretty."

"Very nice." Matt placed his hand on Faith's shoulder and admired the holiday decoration. "Mommy did a wonderful job."

"It's much the same as last year." Lucinda eyed the tree and considered her comment. Somehow, it tied into yesterday's chat with Cynthia. *I'm in a rut.*

"I'll be back." Faith hustled from the room.

Matt looked in the direction his daughter had scampered to. "What's that about?"

"Who knows? Want to sit for a while?" Lucinda stepped toward the sofa.

Matt took a seat beside her. He glanced at her dainty gold hoop earrings, and took in the rest of face. A crease linked her eyebrows together. "Is everything alright? You seem preoccupied."

"I'm fine." She waved her hand in the air. "I've just been analyzing myself."

"Aha, in what ways?"

Faith entered the room and interrupted. "I have presents for you and Daddy." She laid two small square boxes adorned with snowman paper under the tree.

"Where did you get those? I don't recall taking you shopping." Lucinda frowned.

"When we went to get Grandma's tree, me and Grandma bought 'em."

"I remember." Matt nodded. "They wouldn't tell me a thing, just came home with a bag from the gift shop and disappeared for a while."

"Daddy, we had to wrap 'em." Faith sat back on her heels. Her face gleamed at completing her surprise.

"That was nice of your mother." Lucinda watched her daughter place the packages under the tree.

"I'll tell her you said that." Matt addressed Lucinda and then looked at Faith. "Thank you for the gifts. Mommy and I can't wait to open them. Do you mind if I talk to Mommy, alone?"

Faith walked to the couch and hugged him. "Will I see you in church tomorrow?"

"I'll save a seat saved for you." He touched the end of Faith's nose with a love tap, and watched her gather her art pencils and leave.

"So, you were saying something about analyzing." He scooted near. "What's gotten you preoccupied?"

She turned to face him. "Have you ever thought about how you appear to people?"

"Not really." He twisted his mouth. "I imagine others do see us differently than we picture ourselves." Matt laid his hand on Lucinda's knee. "Has someone upset you?"

"Cynthia and I were talking last night. She brought my attention to the fact that since I've lived here I've shied away from relationships." She glanced at Matt, and then quickly tuned her head to the blinking lights on the tree. "I may have, but I don't understand why."

"Well." Matt put his arm around her shoulders. "Do you believe that God has always had a plan for your life?"

"Of course," She gave him a half grin.

"I do too, but I've been stubborn. The Lord had to help me see things in a different perspective."

"I don't understand what that has to do with me not wanting a relationship."

"Don't you?" Matt leaned to her and lightly kissed her. "Dad says the Lord put you in Sonya's life for a reason. On that, I agree. As for me, I messed up big time when I was with her. I was in lust, not in love." He reached for her hand and enclosed it inside his. "God didn't hold my sin against Faith. He gave her a beautiful, caring mother. The Lord also continued to be longsuffering, until time was right for me to repent, and be a good father."

"I can see where the Lord has worked in your life. He brought you back home." Lucinda took a long breath.

"Yes, for more than one reason." He caressed her hand. "Have you given any thought to us? I certainly don't intend to speculate on God's design, but He may have matched us together a long time ago. Things happen in His time."

Matt lifted her head when she looked down at their clasped hands. "I can't imagine my life without you in it." He chuckled and moved his hand, nervously touching his fingers together. "I'm glad you're not involved with another man, because I love you."

"Matt." Lucinda turned toward him and welcomed his embrace. "I suppose the Lord was easing me through the years for a special reason. I've realize that I love you too."

He kissed her once again. After their lips parted, Matt smiled. "I hope this isn't too soon, but I know we can have a wonderful life together, the three of us. Lucinda, will you do me the honor of being my wife."

He held his breath. Lucinda wet her lips and eyed the Christmas tree. He waited, sure that the silence would rip out his ear drums. He exhaled, "Lucinda, I promise to be a good husband, but if you need more time..."

As his words filled the room Lucinda closed the short distant between them. She kissed him with the passion she'd longed to show weeks ago. "I'd be proud to be your wife." Her eyes crinkled with happiness, before she tenderly touched Matt's face, "But I'd like us to talk to Pastor Lamoure. I know he'll be our ally. I want him to marry us, and also to know Faith's story."

"You've made me a happy man." He took her hand in his. "When I was in Washington I confided in him. I'll call, and make an appointment for us to speak to him privately.

· · ❧ · ·

SIX MONTHS, AND SPRING came to Black Mountain. The trees and flowers were joining the happy couple in a promise of a new beginning. Matt stood at the front of the church and fidgeted the same way he had months before, when he'd admitted his love to Lucinda. His mom wiped a tear from her cheek. He chuckled low. *Women cry at everything.* He'd tab that in his memory to use in his latest manuscript.

The piano played while his mind turned the pages back to Thanksgiving, and the day that changed his life.

He glanced out the side window at the blossoms that seemed heaven-sent, from spring's sunshine. "Thank you Lord, for my daughter, and my beautiful bride."

The music changed its beat. Matt stiffened. He lovingly looked at the flower girl. Prettiest little girl he'd ever seen. *My Princess.* Faith ambled up the aisle tossing pedals. Her mouth spread with cheer. She reached the front row and took a seat beside Grandma and Grandpa.

Tunes from the bridal march filled the church. Everyone stood. Matt couldn't take his eyes off his beautiful bride. Her silky gown, with one side resting off her shoulder, and the flowery lace made her black hair shine. She would soon be his wife.

"I do." His steady breath stretched out words that meant everything to him while he placed the diamond band on Lucinda's finger.

Matt swallowed to soothe his dry throat. This moment would define him. Seeing his book titles on the best sellers' list paled in comparison to becoming Lucinda's husband.

"To have and to hold." With a husband's longing, he gazed at Lucinda, as she affirmed their commitment.

"You may kiss the bride." The preacher's words settled around him.

Matt kissed her with what he hoped was an assurance for enduring passion that would last the rest of their lives.

The Church leader looked at the guests. "Friends, the book of Genesis 2:18, says, 'And the LORD God said, [It is] not good that the man should be alone; I will make him an help meet for him.'" He held out his hand toward Matt and Lucinda. "I present to you Mr. and Mrs. Matthew Blake. God bless their union."

The end

About the Author

MARY L. BALL IS A MULTI-published Christian author. Some of her novels include Escape to Big Fork Lake, Redemption in Big Fork Lake and Sparks of Love. She resides in North Carolina.